THIS WAY OUT

A novel

Dedicated to the memory of some
of those for whom The Sixties
were swinging in only one
direction.

by

Louise Darby

Acknowledgements

I would like to thank Marianne Hulse and Alec Rapkin
for their help in bringing this book into being.

All proceeds from the sale of this book will go to Age UK.

THIS WAY OUT

All the characters in this story
are purely fictional.

© 2015 Louise Darby

Contents

Chapter 1	1
Chapter 2	8
Chapter 3	21
Chapter 4	33
Chapter 5	39
Chapter 6	45
Chapter 7	58
Chapter 8	67
Chapter 9	77
Chapter 10	89
Chapter 11	95
Chapter 12	101
Chapter 13	110
Chapter 14	122
"The Union"	128

Chapter 1

Week after week the cold, wet spring of 1983 gloomed across the Midlands. Only now and then did a pale sun shine briefly, tantalising with its promise of better days to come. It was on one such afternoon of transitory brightness that a man in his early thirties drove through the main entrance of Delton Community Hospital.

Turning into one of the few empty spaces in the car park, he noted that this now extended across the entire frontage of the grounds. It had replaced the medley of small buildings, shrubs and stone walls which he remembered.

The once narrow approach lane climbing up to the hospital had also been widened into an obviously busy thoroughfare. The main gardens seemed to be still intact, but a big lawn which had formerly adjoined them had disappeared beneath a two-storey brick building, connected by a glass-sided corridor to the older block which he had known as the nerve-centre of the former Moortop Hospital and Welfare Home.

On the slight rise of ground in the heart of the complex stood the original structure of the old workhouse and its hospital wing, the grey stones proclaiming a history and a permanence of spirit which would never be matched by the rash of newer buildings surrounding them.

A proliferation of signs and notices tended initially to confuse rather than clarify but Dr Brookes, well-accustomed to extracting essentials of information, was soon following the directions leading him to the administrative section. He found himself in an entrance lobby in what had once been part of the welfare accommodation, now modernised and refurbished into offices.

Through a glass partition in the wall facing him he

could see a number of desks, a telephone console, a small word-processor. He touched the button marked "Reception" and a young woman slid back a panel in the glass.

"Afternoon. Can I help?"

"Yes, I'm Dr Brookes. I wonder, do a Mrs Grace Morley or Mrs Beryl Grant by any chance still work here?" he asked.

The receptionist called across the room.

 "Grace, it's someone for you."

 She turned back to the window.

"We've no Mrs Grant here now. I think she left about eight or nine years ago – before I came, anyway."

A door opened at the far end of the wall and a woman of about sixty came out, looking enquiringly at the visitor.

"Hello, Mrs Morley."

She peered up at him through her spectacles.

"I'm sorry, I don't think..."

"Surely I haven't changed that much, have I Grace?"

Grace Morley took off her glasses and brushed back a strand of hair.

"It's Martin, isn't it? Martin Brookes? Good grief, what a surprise! Long time no see with a vengeance!"

The dated phrases encapsulated so precisely for Martin the remembered character of the woman whose hand he was now shaking that his first shock on registering how unexpectedly old and weary she looked quickly passed, and it seemed inconceivable that fifteen years had elapsed since he had last seen her.

"I was passing through this way from the north and thought I'd look the old place up and see what changes time had wrought," he said, smiling to himself at his pedantic phrase – a subconscious counter to her own?

"Quite a lot, as I expect you've seen on your way in – not to mention my grey hair and wrinkles." Grace turned to the young woman who stood listening with frank curiosity.

"This young man worked here for a few months when he was even younger than you, Jackie," she said. "I'll take him over to the staff room for some tea – you can call me there if anything urgent crops up."

She moved towards the outer door, and Martin followed.

"I expect you could drink a cuppa, couldn't you? The old canteen's long gone but we do a nice line in self-service in the new staff room these days."

As they made their way through the corridors Grace pointed out the new extensions and changed functions of various areas which had been effected over the years. They arrived in what Martin recognised as having been the residents' dining hall, transformed into a comfortable if somewhat utilitarian eating-cum-recreation area. A false ceiling concealed the beamed roof, and a system of light-coloured panelled room dividers reduced the large space to units of varying size.

"All in the cause of progress, of course," said Grace. "Personally, I was upset at losing our lovely old hall, but admittedly it did become a bit of a white elephant after the residents went. You should've seen the poor old things, crying and carrying on – you can imagine some of them, can't you? Moortop had been home to some of them for much of their lives, when all's said and done."

They carried their cups to a low table near one of the tall windows. Grace lit a cigarette, and then held out the packet to Martin.

"I don't suppose you smoke?"

He smiled. "No, and you should know better after all your years in a hospital. I don't remember you as a smoker?"

"I started when Roger was killed – but that's another story. I won't bore you with it." She inhaled deeply.

"I'm so sorry, Grace – I had no idea. I'm completely

out of touch with Delton news these days, since my parents left. If you'd rather not talk about it..."

Grace shook her head.

"No, it's all right. It happened two years ago last summer – I'm just about getting over it now, if you can ever say you do get over a thing like that. We were on holiday in Greece. There was a boating accident and Roger was drowned. Pretty shattering experience, but it's quite true what people say, time does heal to some extent, at least. Now, what about you? Where are you working now? How are your parents? Are you married?"

"Heavens, what an interrogation... Well, now, where to begin? I didn't come back to Delton much during my training, and not at all once I'd started in practice, except to help Mum and Dad when they moved. I'm working in the East End now – a three-partner practice. Very hard work, stupidly long hours and totally unglamorous, but rewarding in ways I'd never have dreamed of when I began training. I'm specialising in geriatrics – psycho geriatrics particularly. I do two sessions a week in one of the local hospitals. And on reflection, I think it probably all started with poor old Zoe Trimmer – d'you remember that day when her son arrived out of the blue and you took me over to the old hut?"

Grace smiled, but her eyes were sad.

"Yes, I certainly do remember. You were only a kid then, Martin, and I never said anything at the time, but – don't mock me, will you? – I know I went home that night and thought: if I'd had a son I'd have wanted him to be something like you."

Martin said nothing. He sipped at his tea. Grace stubbed out her cigarette. Both were recalling the unlikely relationship they had once known, the mutual understanding and respect which had never been openly expressed but which had been significant for them both.

"What happened to Zoe in the end?" asked Martin.

"She died – not long after you left Delton. Her son was trying to make arrangements to get her to Canada, if you remember. It never came to anything, though."

Again there was a little silence, broken by Grace.

"Where did your parents go when your Dad retired? Devon, wasn't it? Are they OK?"

"Yes thanks, they're fine. They've got a bungalow not far from Brixham. Dad's a new man since they moved! You know he had a mild heart attack and that's why he retired early? Now what about all the changes here – you'd hardly recognise most of it as the old Moortop, I must say."

"We've still got two of the original wards for the old dears, but the other beds are general now. There's a small casualty, and we've got our own pharmacy and a lot of out-patient clinics and various other services. But development is at a standstill now, with the money situation being what it is."

"And you, Grace, are you still doing the same job here?"

"Actually, since you ask, I ought to charge you fifty pence to talk to me – or at least demand an appointment. I'm the assistant administrator."

"Really? I'm duly honoured." He joined in her game, instinctively understanding her need to play it. "Oh yes, one piece of news you'll be interested in, I'm in close touch again with Margaret Bennett. In fact we're jointly writing a text-book. Although she's retired, she hasn't lost interest."

"Those were the days, eh? I sometimes really hanker after the way it used to be here. Good luck with the book, anyway. And remember me to Margaret when you see her, won't you." She looked at her watch.

"Sorry Martin, I'll have to be getting back. In spite of all the changes there's no let-up in the work load. It's still like Paddy's market most of the time – that's no different. Never mind, only another six months to go and I'll be saying my fond farewells here, after twenty-five years."

"You mean you're retiring?"

Grace nodded.

"Yes, believe it or not I shall be sixty in October. If you're round this way again on the thirty-first, come and join the party. I mean to have a real rave-up for my last fling here – go out in style."

Martin felt a surge of genuine affection for this woman who seemed still in many ways, as they used to say of some of his own generation, a "crazy mixed-up kid", but whose courage and compassion he could still recognise and admire. And now she was widowed and facing her own old age alone.

"Is it all right if I have a wander round before I go? Do I have to have anyone's permission?"

"No, that'll be OK, I'm sorry I haven't time to come with you – the burdens of office, and all that! But I'll ring the wards and let them know you're on your way – though I don't think there are many of the staff still here from your day."

"Thanks." He paused, then: "Here – let me give you my address and phone number, and if you're ever in London, look me up. It's only a bachelor flat, but..." He laughed at her quizzical expression, which even now had a hint in it of her old bawdiness. "No, I'm not married – not yet, that is."

He gave her the slip of paper and took her hand.

"It's been grand seeing you again," he said. "Take care of yourself, Grace, and if it helps – although I think you know anyway – I'd just like to remind you that you helped to set one young man on the road to a very worthwhile destination about fifteen years ago, and he won't ever forget it."

Grace dragged her free hand across her eyes, then snatched the other from his grasp. She replaced her spectacles.

"Get away with you!" She grinned, but her lip was

trembling. "See you sometime, Martin," and she was gone.

As he walked round the hospital he saw much that he itched to comment on, to challenge, despite the many changes which had been made since he was last here. He made several mental notes of points to discuss with Margaret. What a long way there was still to go in this field, he thought, and what an endlessly uphill journey it sometimes seemed. In your teens, even in your twenties, you dreamed of righting wrongs overnight, and if necessary, single-handed. In your thirties you began to see that it might not perhaps be that easy but you didn't give up trying.

Back in the car park he took a last look round before starting his engine and then, following the sign directing "This Way Out", he headed for London.

Chapter 2

"Is that you, Martin?"

Edna switched off the portable radio as she heard the front door close. Martin came into the kitchen, dropping a duffel bag and placing his clarinet case carefully beside it.

"And who else would it be letting themselves in through the front door at this time of day?" He grinned. "Hello Mum."

He reached for one of the shortbreads Edna had just taken from the oven, and she tapped his wrist.

"No picking. You'll spoil your meal. How did today's practice go?"

"Rehearsal, please – we're not a village choir. I'd have you know we aim for professional standards in the jazz group!" He pretended a half-challenging, half-hurt expression, then smiled again.

"Oh, not too bad. Colin didn't turn up, though. He's gone for another interview." He kicked a phantom adversary across the floor.

"Well now, I've a bit of news for you. I saw Margaret Bennett in town at lunch-time and there's a temporary job going in the office up at Moortop. The man who normally does it has had some sort of accident and is likely to be off work for quite some time. D'you think it would be worth your while giving them a ring?"

Martin pulled back a chair and sat down, stretched out under the table.

"I suppose it might be. At least it'd mean a bit of cash to help out, but I can't see myself fitting into office work. Hardly a substitute for medical school, is it?"

"No, but at least it's in a hospital – that might be useful experience."

"I don't think I'm likely to learn much about

doctoring in the office of some tin pot little geriatric set-up like Moortop."

Edna turned from the sink and looked at her son. She still found herself being startled by his eighteen-year-old arrogance, even though she knew it concealed a vulnerability, a searching for certainties.

"Oh Martin, humility was never your strong point, was it? You'll get your A levels next time, I'm sure, but in the meantime don't be too bitter. This job, Up the Hill, see what your Dad thinks when he comes in. But I shouldn't leave it too long before you enquire if you're going to. Even though it's temporary I dare say they'll be able to get somebody without too much difficulty."

"I'll think about it. Who's Margaret Bennett, anyway?"

"She's the new Assistant Matron – I've met her a few times now. She's joined the History Society to try to get to know people. Nice person – ideal in that job, I'd say."

Martin stood up, chair legs scraping the floor tiles.

"Right then. What time's Dad coming in? I'm hungry."

Before Edna could answer he was halfway to the stairs, and soon she heard the self-confident stridency of the latest Stan Kenton recording hitting the walls of his bedroom. She bent to pick up the duffel bag and hung it on the hook behind the door, wishing that she didn't find the outlook of Martin and his generation quite so unnerving. Already the phrase "swinging sixties" was common currency; often she thought "shattering" would be a more appropriate adjective.

When, rarely, Martin did voice his views to her and Arnold she was always left with the feeling that nothing was stable any longer; all values were questioned; everything was game for attack; no area of experience barred from exploration for these old-young creatures.

Stan Kenton had blown himself out: she took the

clarinet case to the bottom of the stairs, turning her head to call Martin, but was defeated by the opening bars of an early Beatles offering. She paused to listen. She liked the Beatles... She went back into the kitchen and switched on the radio again. Woman's Hour had long since ended.

"No two days alike in this job, Martin my lad, and you'll never have time to be bored. Isn't that right, Beryl?"

Grace opened the top drawer of her desk and lifted out a folder of notes awaiting typing. She caught a fingernail on the drawer front as she closed it, and swore quietly. From another drawer she took out a manicure wallet and began to file the broken, orange-coloured nail.

Beryl, plump and dark-haired, smiled vaguely at Grace whilst continuing to give her attention to Martin. She was sitting beside him at his desk, checking the entries as he made them in the daily records of patients who had come in, gone out or died during the past twenty-four hours.

This was the middle of his second week, and already he was wondering how long he'd be able to endure this job. Despite the diversions inseparable from any organisation where human beings were the reason for its existence, many of the daily office routines at Moortop were repetitive and Martin, naturally bright, had mastered the simple basics in the first couple of days. He now glanced quickly from Grace to Beryl.

Beryl Grant reminded him of his own mother – conscientious, kind – in fact she too might have made a good infant teacher. He supposed she was around his mother's age – her daughter Angela had been a year senior to him at Barford High. Beryl fussed him a bit, treated him as though he were nearer eight than eighteen, and seemed to think he needed telling a dozen times before he understood anything. Still, she meant well, he felt, and – saving grace! (grinning to himself at the pun) – didn't try to include him in the trivial small talk which went on for much of the time between the two women when they weren't actually nose-to-grindstone.

Grace Morley was another kettle of fish entirely. If I don't stick it out, he thought, blotting the last entry carefully and closing the register as Beryl stood up to go back to her own desk, it'll be more than likely because of Grace. If only she'd act her age... she must be well over forty; why couldn't she see that trying to project the image of a rider on the current swinging bandwagon only made her look like a prize fool? That brassy blonde hair; it might be fashionable but, like her clothes, the style was far too young for her. And such clothes on such a short, squat frame – almost grotesque.

The phone rang. Grace answered it, and he listened to her cliché-peppered end of the conversation. Despite the brief time he'd known her he was sure he could have made a fairly accurate inventory of her household possessions without ever having visited her home; and he wouldn't mind betting that he'd recognise her estate-agent husband Roger, whom he'd never met, if he saw him in a crowded street.

More than half the morning was already gone before Martin was able to get across to the canteen for his coffee. Beryl and Grace, he had learned, chose to stay at their desks during their breaks, sharing local gossip and flasks of morning coffee (supplied by Grace) and afternoon tea (by Beryl). This custom had obviously hardened into law over the years they'd worked together.

His desk was near to the side window and he could look out over the large main lawns and gardens towards the wooded area on the far boundary, beyond which lay open countryside. To his right he could see the visitors' gate and it was early that afternoon when he noticed a middle-aged man just inside the grounds, looking uncertainly about him. His bearing and the cut of his clothes suggested subtly that he was not English.

"I think somebody's lost out there," he said. "Shall I go and see?"

Grace got up from her desk.

"Amazing how few people seem to be able to read," she said. "You'd think there wasn't a sign in the place. Why don't they look at the direction boards? Where is he, anyway?"

She moved over to the window and gave a girlish shriek.

"Oh, I say, isn't he a dish? Stay where you are, Martin, I bags this one."

Martin winced in embarrassment. He watched as she smoothed down the ridiculously short skirt. She licked her forefingers and drew them across her eyebrows before going out of the office.

He stared out of the window.

The dull October afternoon hinted at winter. In the rose beds beyond the top lawn a few late blooms, their petals brown-edged, dripped the last of the morning's shower onto the soil.

As Grace walked back with the visitor she was talking animatedly, and then they passed from Martin's view as they went up the stairs behind the office, presumably to Mr Barraclough's room on the floor above.

About five minutes later she came back into the office and closed the door.

"What did I tell you about no two days being alike, Martin? I've taken our Canadian friend up to have a word with the Hospital Secretary before we go any further. He wants permission to find out from the records what he can about his mother. He thinks he was born here just after the First World War. Come on, Martin. This is your chance to be introduced to our history department."

She took a ring of keys from a box in her drawer and turned to Beryl.

"Shan't be long, Beryl, but if we're not back in twenty minutes you'd better send someone to rescue me from a fate worse than death."

She grinned at Martin as she spoke and again he flinched inwardly. The incongruity of her behaviour embarrassed him far more than her mock suggestiveness.

They went out into the damp chill of the afternoon and he followed her down the side of the office block and round to the rear of the main buildings. They crossed a yard just inside the boundary wall to reach a wooden hut standing in a corner of the grounds.

"This was put up during the war," Grace told him. "It was used then as some kind of emergency accommodation. It was never taken down, and we keep all the old records and some out of date equipment in it now. It's quite a little museum, as you'll see."

They climbed three wooden steps, and Grace unlocked the door and switched on the light. The musty smell breathed at them out of the past. Shelving ran the length of one wall, packed closely with files and books, boxes and bundles of papers. At the far end of the hut pieces of old furniture gathered dust. A Victorian bath-chair, a zinc hip-bath and other relics lined the wall opposite the shelves, and in one corner were stacks of old heavy frames. Martin caught sight of texts and faded photographs showing through the grime and resolved to make an early opportunity to come back again when he could be alone to examine at his leisure this accumulation of Moortop's history.

Grace was searching the shelves at the far end of the wall.

"Here, Martin, give me a hand, kid. We need the register for 1918 or 1919. It should be somewhere in this section – we'll have a look at it here before we decide whether to take it over to the office. You never know what you're going to find out when you open one of these. In any case, remember all the stuff in these records is strictly confidential, and they're not to be shown to every Tom, Dick or Harry who might ask to see them. Ah, here we are!"

She lifted down a large bound volume, on the spine of which were the words: "The Admission and Discharge Book", and underneath the gilt letters a hand-written label read: "Delton Union, April 1916 to December 1919".

Martin took the book from her and carried it to the rickety card-table standing in the middle of the hut, where he flicked off the dust with his sleeve. Grace opened the cover and looking over her shoulder he glimpsed "Poor Law Boards... Workhouse Regulations..." on the inner title page.

The thick leaves were set out in columns similar to those he had been working on that morning, but here the script was near to genuine copper-plate, and the printed headings were significantly different, as was the nature of some of the information contained in them. No longer these days was it necessary to record "Number affixed to inmate's clothing", nor did any "Observation on condition at time of admission" reveal details like "Vagrant" or "verminous". He was glad, too, that any entries he might have to make were unlikely to include such depressing conclusions to a period in Moortop as "hanged himself" or "discharged on the Master's orders for refusing to work".

Grace searched for several minutes, while Martin let his imagination whirl around the bare facts set down all those decades before, fleshing out the skeletons of the stark details with his mental images of the characters they represented.

"This looks hopeful." Grace was pointing to an entry at the head of a page, the ink faded to a pale grey-brown, but still clearly legible.

"It wasn't only tramps and vagabonds who came in in those days, you know. A lot of kids were born here.

Their mothers were fallen women, or abandoned wives, or whatever. It looks as if Mr Broadbent's mother might have been one of them."

Martin looked at the page where she pointed.

> Thurs. 2.10.19. Trimmer, Zoe. Domestic servant. C. of E. Born 1.2.00. Fem. No.129. Admitted from Parish of Ashwell Dale.

and underneath:

> Fri. 3.10.19. Trimmer, Luke. Child. Born 3.10.19. Name of Parent, Zoe.

"What do we do now?" Martin asked, as Grace stood silent, her finger still marking the entry. She didn't answer and he looked at her face in the dim light of the low-powered bulb. For a brief moment he saw a different Grace from the woman he knew. The moment passed, but he knew he would recall it again and again.

"To be perfectly honest, Martin, I don't quite know. I think I'd better have a word with Mr Barraclough before we go any further. I wonder if he's still got the chappie with him? I'll go over to a phone and find out. You lock up and go back to the office – leave the register there – we'll probably need it again. If Mr Broadbent's in the office when you get back, don't let on that we've found anything."

When she had gone, Martin read the entry again. If this was the record of Luke Broadbent's birth he now had a different name, might be illegitimate, but whether or not he knew that, why should Grace seem so disturbed? She was a strange mixture – trying to pretend she treated life as all fun and games, and yet patently caring about Moortop and its inhabitants, knowing most of them by name and as much about some of their histories as if they'd been her own relatives.

He turned back to the book. "Zoe Trimmer". The unusual name rang a bell. He thought he'd heard one of the Sisters talking in the office about a patient with that name, on her ward now. Surely it wasn't possible that she could be this man's mother, here in Moortop, nearly fifty years after she'd been taken in to have her baby? He turned over some more pages, and saw that a few days later in that long-ago October Zoe Trimmer and her child had left Delton Union "at her own request, in the care of a friend".

He switched off the light and locked the door.

In the far corner of the office Grace was talking quietly to Sister Fellowes when Martin got back.

"The dates of birth certainly tally with the information he's already got, and both their Christian names – neither of them exactly common; but of course he's always known his surname as Broadbent, having been adopted when he was only a few weeks old. The Broadbents apparently knew Zoe as child. They took Luke over and went to live in Birmingham, then emigrated to Canada in the mid-twenties, so he doesn't remember much about this country at all."

Sister Fellowes looked thoughtful.

"How much does he know about his natural mother?"

"He told Mr Barraclough that when he was old enough – about sixteen, I think he said – his parents told him that he'd been born in Delton and that his mother couldn't look after him, so they adopted him. Not much more, it seems. They're both dead now – the father died last year – and he decided to have a trip over here to find out what he could..."

She stopped speaking as the Hospital Secretary came into the office together with the visitor and Margaret Bennett.

"Mrs Morley, would you take Mr Broadbent over to the hut and let him look at the register, please?" said Mr

Barraclough. "And then he'd like to go up onto the ward to see Miss Trimmer."

Then Miss Bennett spoke to Luke Broadbent.

"While you're over at the hut, Sister will try to explain to Miss Trimmer that she's got a visitor, but as we've said, she is very confused and it seems unlikely she'll understand much of what's happening. She's in a side ward on her own at the moment, so you can be quite private. Just let Sister know if you'd like her to be with you, and if there's anything more we can do to help, you have only to ask."

She stood back to let them leave, and turned to Martin.

"You're Edna Brookes' son, aren't you? I'm glad you've joined us here for a little while. It's a good thing to have some people of your age around – it cheers the patients to see a young man's face now and again.

Martin smiled his response as she went out.

When he and Beryl were alone he asked:

"Do you think Zoe Trimmer really is that man's mother?"

"It seems pretty certain. What a sad visit it will be for him. Poor Miss Trimmer just isn't with it at all, you know. She's the one who sits all day folding up paper and bits of cloth. The staff keep giving it to her all crumpled up so she can smooth it out. Do you remember seeing her when you came round with me on Friday?"

He nodded.

"I wonder what he'll do?"

He tried to imagine how he'd feel if he suddenly found out that the woman he knew as his mother wasn't really his mother at all, as this chap had done when he was little younger than himself. Probably if you were happy and got on well with the people you'd grown up with, it might not affect everyday life all that much. But deep inside? Surely all sorts of disturbances, questions, would came with such a discovery, whether or not you decided to take much notice of them, let them influence you. And what about not knowing who or where your real father was? If Luke Broadbent had had in mind for thirty years the idea of tracing his history and had now travelled thousands of miles to follow that intention through, he must have been deeply affected.

He and Beryl had almost finished their day's work and were clearing their desks when Grace came back. She was like another person again. In place of the usual superficial inanity her demeanour was serious, and her voice quiet.

"Poor devil. There's little doubt he is Zoe's son. You can even see the likeness when they're together. I've left him on the ward with Mary Fellowes, and what he must be feeling now God alone knows. Obviously he can't stay in England to be near her – he's got a responsible job in Canada, to say nothing of a wife and two kids. And just as clearly he can't take the old woman out of here just like that and drag her over there, even if he wants to."

They were all silent for a few minutes, thinking of the strange meeting taking place only a short distance away from them. Suddenly Grace's mood changed yet again. She began to whistle as she cleared her desk briskly. Then she said:

"Well, I shan't get this lot done now until tomorrow. Lucky there's nothing urgent – I'm certainly not staying on to do any more tonight. We're going out to dinner at the Broadlands with Geoff and Anthea. Come on Martin, don't stand about looking like a drowned duck in a thunderstorm. These things do happen, you know. Makes life interesting, doesn't it? I said you'd never be bored here. 'Night, everybody."

She was gone, and while Beryl checked the locks Martin collected up the mail to post in the town. They walked across the yard in the thickening damp of the early evening, Beryl as always hurrying in front to get home to prepare her family's meal.

Martin called "Goodnight" as she went out of sight. He walked slowly down the dark lane leading towards the main road into Delton. Luke Broadbent must be in the devil of a state, he thought. He hadn't reappeared in the office, although he'd said he would call back again tomorrow with some kind of decision or suggested arrangements about Zoe Trimmer's future. Martin didn't envy him his thoughts and feelings on this dreary autumn night in a lonely room in Delton's one rather comfortless hotel.

As he walked on, he began to piece together what he'd learned of Zoe's life. Born in a village in one of the more remote and bleak areas of the county she'd gone into service in her early teens. The records, of course, said nothing about the man who, four or five years later, had fathered her illegitimate child, neither were the years following her discharge after her son's birth documented anywhere. So until today, Martin realised, no-one would have had any reason to connect the admission in the 1950s of an old woman to "welfare" with that of a young girl in labour fifty years before.

She'd been brought in when her small rented cottage on the outskirts of Delton had been destroyed by fire, and with it all her meagre possessions. Local hearsay and her own sparse accounts had revealed that for years she'd been scraping a living by doing domestic work in some of the big houses, but as she'd grown older and unable to walk the considerable distances involved, this employment had petered out and her health had deteriorated. The fire had affected her mental balance and she had, since coming back to Moortop, rarely spoken to anyone, staff or other residents. In the end, physically frail and totally withdrawn, she'd been taken onto Linnet Ward where Martin had first seen her.

The image of the tiny white-haired, dark-eyed figure sitting alone, her shaking hands forever smoothing out and folding crumpled cloth or paper seemed to illustrate for Martin the perplexity he'd experienced since he'd worked at Moortop. Before, he'd never visited the far country which to him, was old age. Now, in less than two weeks, he'd been confronted not only with many of its sights, sounds and smells but also with some of the less tangible elements which made up that distant land, and had been made by turns curious, embarrassed and occasionally depressed by its foreignness. What was it really like, for example, to be a Zoe, apparently oblivious to even the most basic human needs – food, drink, communication?

He reached the main post-office, dropped the mail into the box and turned towards home.

"Hullo, dear. How's it gone today?"

His mother was carefully stirring a thickening sauce, her back to him. He bent over and pecked at her cheek – a gesture rare enough to cause her to drop the spoon into the pan. She fished it out.

"Very interesting day, Mum. I think I've learned quite a lot, as a matter of fact."

"That's some admission from you, Martin. Dinner won't be long. We won't wait for your father – he's on late rota this evening. Have you got a practice – sorry, rehearsal – tonight?"

"There is one, but I shan't go. There's some reading I want to do. In fact I might think about giving up the group for a bit. Better concentrate on some revision and get good grades next time round. There seems to be more point..."

He broke off. Edna decided not to comment. I'm learning too, she thought, and smiled at his retreating back as he went up to wash.

Chapter 3

Even at her interview Margaret Bennett had suspected that she might find herself on a different wavelength from Matron Gifford. Twice during that occasion she had tried to tune in to areas more subtle than those simply concerned with conventional nursing care; twice Irene Gifford had politely but determinedly switched the direction of the conversation. Margaret had had little hope of response – and had achieved none – from the lay member of the interviewing panel, but she had noticed a raised eyebrow of interest on Dr Rayner's face, and when offered the post she had accepted it, despite some misgivings.

That was three months ago – time enough to convince her that neither personal nor professional problems at Moortop were going to be easily solved.

"Do you want me to go round this morning, Matron?"

Miss Gifford consulted the desk diary.

"Yes, I suppose you'd better. I can't be in two places at once, and this meeting with Mr Barraclough is sure to drag on, knowing him. Bring your report over to the flat at lunchtime, then I can deal with any queries before the House Committee at two o'clock."

Margaret gathered up the duty books and turned to leave the tiny office. The sliding panel of the cupboard near the door was only slightly open, but that was sufficient for anyone coming into the room to be able to glimpse a gin bottle inadequately concealed on the top shelf. She quietly slid the panel shut as she passed.

At the entrance to Robin Ward kitchen she edged round a trolley being loaded with cutlery and crockery. She greeted the two domestics and marked off their names on the rota. The main corridor as she approached appeared chaotic. In fact she knew there were ordered patterns controlling this slow-moving rush-hour of old people going to and from bath and lavatory, day-room and beds, their motive power a jumble of wheelchairs, walking frames, sticks and nurses' arms.

The duty room was empty, and seeing Sister at the far end of the ward she went towards her.

"Everyone on who should be, Sister?"

Sister Hemsley looked up, weariness – even this early in the day – showing through her smile.

"Yes, Miss Bennett, but, as usual it's not enough."

"Have you got time to report, or shall I leave you to it and come back later?"

"No, I've finished here for the moment, thank you. We're expecting an admission any time now – Emma Naylor from Bankside Cottages – so we'll probably have our hands full for the rest of the morning."

On each of the wards Margaret was met with the same reserved politeness – a distance in manner which was surely more than could be explained simply by respect for her office?

The wards themselves, bright and fresh, spoke of a tradition of unremitting and largely successful efforts to eradicate the old image of workhouses and unions. Moortop had much in its favour, decided Margaret, but the faces of the patients, so many portraits of isolation and withdrawal, were to her mind visible evidence of the paradoxes which troubled her.

She moved outside again, across the inner yards to the oldest part of the buildings, still called "The House", now occupied by a resignation of women and men who had been forced, for a variety of reasons, to come in from the cold of a society with which they could no longer cope, to the shelter of "welfare". Though a few of them teetered perilously on the edge of total dependence most were still comparatively whole in mind and body. The vital light that was all but extinguished in the sick on the wards still flashed erratically in these faces.

Pathetically, those who clung to the remnants of their self-patterns strove, as she passed, to demonstrate to her their frail victory.

"Seein' the boy-friend tonight are we, then?" Martha was staring at Margaret's newly-styled hair, a leer glimmering grotesquely in her tiny blue eyes.

Anne Prince, simpering, expensive rings loose on shrunken fingers, offered a sticky sweet from a crumpled paper bag.

An attempt at a wolf-whistle drew her attention to Eddie's ill-fitting dentures.

"Now then, Eddie, mind your manners." She moved on.

"Good morning, Joe. Are you going out for a walk today?" Joe Bird shook his head, his habitual armour of reserve remaining undented.

She made her way to the staff kitchen, where she found Harriet Frost, the attendant in charge of the section, drinking tea with her assistant, Mrs Blake. As she approached she could hear their whining exchanges of criticism about the residents, which stopped abruptly as she went in.

"Good morning, Miss Bennett." Both women stood up.

She returned their greeting, ensuring by her tone that they should realise she had heard at least part of their conversation.

"Miss Frost, I notice Eddie Thompson's dentures seem to be giving him trouble. Will you arrange for a dental visit, please?"

"Of course, I'll see to it straight away. As a matter of fact I'd had it in mind for a week or two, but we've been so busy..."

Margaret cut her off.

"You might do a check round and see if there's anyone else needing treatment while you're about it, and make all the appointments together."

"Yes, I'll do that. Anything else, Miss Bennett?"

Was there a hint of insolence, or did she only hear it because of her doubts about Harriet Frost's attitude to the job?

Walking back towards Matron's office she saw an ambulance coming through the main gate. She turned back towards the hospital. Sister Hemsley would probably welcome a bit of help if that was Emma Naylor coming in. She was delayed by two or three other encounters and the new patient was already in bed when she reached the ward.

"How does she seem?"

Margaret went closer to the bed. The old woman seemed to be asleep, although her lips were moving. She bent her head, trying to hear, but whatever Emma was saying was for herself alone. Margaret and the Sister walked quietly away.

"Keep an eye on her, Sister, and let me know what Doctor says when he's seen her, will you?"

Cold, Emma remembered, awareness gradually returning – cold, and stiffness, and a peculiar emptiness at the centre of her self. No pain, no sudden sharp assault had brought her down...

"No pain?"

The voice – distant – behind blankets of fog, slowly clearing.

"Any pain anywhere, Mrs Naylor?"

The voice, again, insistent... Matthew? But he would have said "Emma". Even through the mist she'd realised that. And Matthew could no longer call to her. She'd felt the familiar warmth of tears on her face, lifting a hand to brush them away.

"Try to tell us, Mrs Naylor. Does it hurt anywhere?"

Another voice, equal authority behind it, but female this time. She'd shaken her head slowly, the dizziness swirling inside, and then she'd opened her eyes. Two faces merging, then separating, the bed-rails framing the hazy portrait. Why were they in her bedroom? Who were they? What was she doing on the floor, looking up at strangers?

So much strangeness, so many questions, and she'd felt too tired, too feeble to try to find answers. Gentle hands feeling her limbs, softly lifting her.

"No bones broken it seems, Doctor"

She'd had time to realise as they'd soothed her back onto the bed, that help had finally come; that the weeks of lonely, desperate worrying since she had watched Matthew die in this same bed, were over; that Doctor Hogden and the grey-uniformed woman with him would not leave her to die alone, in the shabby neglected room which she had been unable, to her regret, any longer to keep neat and bright. But how had they found her? Had she left the back door open when she had come upstairs?

"Stay with her, Nurse, while I go and telephone for an ambulance."

Apprehension shivering through her once more at the implication of the words, and then darkness again.

Another bed, harder now, and no comforting rose-covered eiderdown but a plain counterpane, the sunshine a pale golden path crossing the whiteness. Elusive images came and went, of a hushed dark ride, all sense of direction lost, lying on her back and seeing a blue dim square of window that revealed nothing; of another ride, still on her back, along high-ceilinged corridors into a lift; more corridors...

"Good afternoon, Mrs Naylor. How are you feeling now?"

She turned her head and was looking into a smiling face, shiny black, the dark eyes friendly behind large spectacles. She remembered vaguely a time long in the past when she had wondered what her reaction would be should she ever need to be cared for by so alien a pair of hands. The nurse was deftly smoothing the pillow, easing Emma's aching back up the bed into a more comfortable position.

"Is that better, Mrs Naylor? Now, would you maybe like something to drink before Doctor comes to have a look at you?"

"Thank you, no, I'll wait a little. You're very kind. Where am I then?"

"You're all right, Mrs Naylor. We'll look after you, flower. You'll soon feel at home with us. This is Moortop, you know?"

The unfamiliar accent, the sing-song throaty voice, the pale pink palms of the black-backed hands, prolonged Emma's sense of bewilderment, but she sank back unresisting, recognising competence and kindness to which she could gratefully respond. Her bed and her person were straightened into a neat entity to await the Doctor's arrival.

Moortop, the hospital of the old Union, the workhouse, where the poor and rejected were brought to die! Twenty years and more back she had visited Matthew's mother in a similar institution in Gorley, and the horror of the gloomy hopelessness of the place had lain at the back of her mind ever since. But this was nothing like her memory of Gorley Old People's Hospital. Here, there were pale pink walls and a tinted ceiling, gaily-coloured patterned curtains, and blue and white lino Squares on the floor. Her recollection of that other ward was of brown, lavatory-tile walls, a faded dingy ceiling and dirty pine varnish on the woodwork. And that smell, the odour of despair, that wasn't here, either.

Matthew's mother had died painfully, and Emma had been indignant at the final humiliation inflicted by poverty on one who had deserved so much more than life had ever given her. How many times I've been angered by injustice, Emma thought; and as she did so, felt some of her old strength and spirit returning so that when Doctor Rayner arrived a short time later he was surprised to find her apparently less frail and failing than Hogden's message had led him to expect.

"Doctor Hogden tells me you had a fall, Mrs Naylor?" His friendly voice and kind expression dispelled much of her earlier apprehension, and the examination which followed further increased her confidence.

"Well now, if you behave yourself and do as you're told, there's no reason why you shouldn't be home again before long." He smiled at her again and turned to the grey-haired woman in a white coat who stood with him.

"What's the social background, Mrs Dean?"

"Her husband died a few weeks back, Doctor. He'd worked at the Burrows Plant in Gorley at one time. There's an only daughter, married and living in New Zealand. We're trying to contact her. No other relatives that we know of. Mrs Naylor doesn't belong in this area originally, and of course she's not been able to tell us much since she was brought in this morning."

The Doctor turned back to Emma.

"Fine, fine. We won't worry you any more for the moment, Mrs Naylor. Just take your tablets and be a good girl, and I'll come and see you again tomorrow, eh?"

Her first reaction to his words was tempered when she looked at his eyes. Probably he didn't realise he sounded patronising. Funny how so many people, particularly professional ones, spoke to you as though you were slow-witted just because you were either old, or not – they thought – "in their class". She watched as he walked briskly to the next bed, his concern already switched from her to the apparently lifeless wisp of a creature who lay in it.

"No other relatives that we know of." Bleak words,

and yet bleak wasn't how she'd have described her life, not up to the time Matthew had died, at least. But now, she supposed, she might at last be facing the reckoning which would give her parents, in whatever other world they might be, the ultimate satisfaction – the I-told-you-so response to the downfall they had always predicted for her when she'd married "beneath her" fifty years before.

She lay unmoving, eyes closed, so that Nurse Hooper, checking on the patients as Doctor Rayner finished his round, took her to be asleep, and passed on.

Years since she'd thought much about her parents and suddenly there they were, almost as though actually sitting by her bed, their pinched, disapproving faces not troubling to conceal their triumph at her present plight. Chapel-goers both, how could they possibly not have seen and welcomed the genuineness and the delight which had been the love between Matthew and herself?

Narrow-mindedness and prejudice had won, and they had never accepted him. Easier to criticise than to understand people different from yourself, even your own parents. Hadn't she been equally smug until she met Matthew? Her lips moved in rueful smile, as Nurse Hooper returned down the ward.

"Pleasant dreams, old dear," she said quietly, but Emma heard only the sound of the band playing the last waltz, and then Matthew offering to see her back to the teacher training college from which she'd sneaked out to go with him to the Burrow's Social Club. He moved to take her hand, tentatively...

She opened her eyes. A nursing auxiliary standing by the bed had touched her.

"Here's your tea, Mrs Naylor. I hope you like shepherd's pie?"

Confused, she tried to recall where she was. Another stranger, tall, bonny, her round face smiling from a shine of chestnut hair, spoke:

"Feeling a little better now, I hope? I've just come to see how you are before I go off duty. Have a good night's rest." She turned and left.

Emma looked enquiringly at the younger woman.

"That was Miss Bennett, the Assistant Matron. She was here when you came in this morning. Now, how about this tea?"

"Thank you." Emma contemplated the tray. "I'll eat what I can," she said.

The young auxiliary, slight, dark, not unlike Elizabeth had been at that age, adjusted the bed tray to a comfortable position and moved on.

How kind all these people were. Trying to raise herself into a sitting position she again felt weak and tired.

She wasn't hungry and although she tried she was unable to manage more than a few mouthfuls. She looked around at the other patients. Some were sitting at a table in the middle of the ward, some, helpless in terminal infirmity, were being fed by the staff. Few were talking, one or two babbling or shouting apparently senseless phrases into the air.

What brings us all to this in the end, she wondered. What kind of forces eat into our beings to reduce us to such mockery of the human existence?

She tried to push away the bed tray and then lay back. The pillows had slipped. Her nightdress had rucked up beneath her. The bedclothes, light as they were, weighed on her bruises. She returned with relief to her memories.

The faces of her mother and father had vanished and she could no longer even recall their features – only her sense of Matthew's comfort and support when the news came that they'd both been killed in a road accident. Although she'd grieved, it hadn't been so much for her own loss that she wept as for what they'd missed of joy and warmth because of their acrimonious and judgmental view of life.

She slept briefly, dreaming of Elizabeth. She was standing on a long sandy beach, John at her side in his New Zealand Air Force uniform, her hands reaching across oceans and continents to touch her mother's cheeks.

"Wakey-wakey, m'dear. Cocktail time."

Sister was holding a small glass containing two or three coloured tablets.

"If you sleep all evening you'll never get off tonight, will you now?"

Her voice was brusque, but the local accent somehow softened the no-nonsense manner.

Emma tried to smile. The weakness was increasing, she felt. What had the Doctor said about going home in a day or two? She'd never be able to manage for herself, not yet. It had been hard enough before this silly fall.

"Thank you, Sister. I'm sorry I couldn't finish my tea – I just wasn't very hungry."

At some time the tray had been taken, the curtains drawn around her, but she'd not noticed. Sister Hemsley and the same young auxiliary – she was like Beth! – helped her onto and off the bedpan. Once again she was tidied up in neat conformity with all the other beds around her. The bed-curtains swished back to the wall.

"I'm off home now – see you in the morning," Sister Hemsley said.

Already some of the other patients were asleep, and the autumn-gold sunshine which had fingered the ward earlier had long since faded. Now a wild wind threw showers against the tall windows, but inside there was a quietness made the more emphatic by the odd shouts and cries which broke it. Once again Emma slipped back, into the more recent past, now.

When Matthew retired, a move from Gorley's grime and dinginess to the tiny terraced cottage at Delton, within a bus-ride of the Dales they'd discovered on their honeymoon, had been made possible by adding their few savings to the little unexpected legacy untouched since her parents' death. Walking the fields and hills with their beloved Labrador; reclaiming the neglected cottage garden; learning together to recognise the wild birds and flowers – she'd often said their autumn was even lovelier than their spring had been.

The ward was now in darkness save for a small lamp in the middle, where the elderly Night Sister sat reading and making notes. Emma wondered fleetingly what time it was. A cry from one of the beds at the far end held an inhuman sound, almost like an animal's howl.

"Guy", she thought, and the barrier between "now" and "then" became ever more faint as she slipped to and fro across it. Matthew was crying as he crouched, cradling poor old Guy's drooping head in his arms, and her tears mingled with his as they knelt there and the dog's body grew cold.

"You never really got over Guy's going, did you Matthew? It was then when you suggested we should each try, whichever one of us went first, to let the gap between our deaths be as short as possible. We didn't believe in anything afterwards, did we? And yet now perhaps, after all, I do. Somehow I can see you, hear you more clearly now than in that first week when I was alone and you kept coming back. My dear, when you went I didn't think I could live one single day without you. But I did, lots of days, all as empty and pointless as each other. Even Elizabeth and John, much as I love them, aren't enough reason to keep on alone. (I'm sorry, Beth dear – I know you'd understand.) Not long now Matthew. Can you hear Guy whining? It's very dark. Shine the light for me, will you love? I can't quite see the path..."

Sister Whittington stood up from her desk and looked towards Emma Naylor's bed. She moved swiftly and quietly across the intervening space and checked the occupant gently and thoroughly, and then lifted the sheet over the face. Before returning to her night station she stood looking down at Emma's body and wondered why she experienced such a feeling of comfort and ease. In a long nursing life she had rarely witnessed a more serene, quiet passing.

"Thank you," she murmured. "I never knew you, but I shall always remember you."

She drew the curtains slowly round the bed and went towards the telephone.

Chapter 4

The little core of enthusiasts, Margaret among them, who had shown indifference to the sudden October gale and rain sat tensed against the chill discomfort of the chapel schoolroom. A young man from the University had been invited to speak to the Delton Historical Society on the subject of Luddite activities in the area, and had proved less than stimulating. The projector failed and the meeting faltered to an early finish.

Edna slipped out before the questions and vote of thanks, to make the tea. The geyser roared disconcertingly in a draught from the window. She put away the surplus cups and saucers whilst she waited for the tea to brew.

Speaker and committe members served, she gave out the half dozen or so other cups and then went over to talk to Laura, who was sitting on her own.

"Have you met Margaret Bennett yet?" she asked.

Laura shook her head, and Edna called across to Margaret.

"This is Laura Hancock – she and I were at school together. Her husband, Alan, teaches at Valley Road..."

Before she could complete the introduction, Laura stood up, putting her cup and saucer on the chair behind her.

She greeted Margaret briefly and turned to Edna.

"Sorry – I must go. I wouldn't have come if there hadn't been a speaker..." Her voice was shaky, and her eyes sought something invisible.

"Are you all right, Laura? You look a bit off-colour."

"It's nothing – I'm a bit jaded. I'll ring you sometime."

"How is Alan's father?"

Laura's reply was inaudible, and touching Edna's arm she moved towards the door, and then turned to say to Margaret:

"Forgive me – perhaps another time..."

Edna looked after her.

"I hope she'll be all right. It's not like Laura to be so distracted. I wonder what's upsetting her."

Margaret was buttoning her raincoat.

"I think I'll be getting back, if you'll excuse me – unless I can give you a hand in the kitchen?"

"No, thanks all the same – I can manage these few. Sorry it's been such a poor meeting – not much chance for you to get to know anybody"

"There'll be other times Mrs Brookes, don't worry. By the way, I met your son this morning. I should think he's a very capable young man, and I'm sure he'll be a great help in the office."

"I hope so. I know he's finding it interesting. Now, I'd better collect up the cups. You've got the date of the next meeting?"

"Yes thanks. Goodnight. "

Martin and his father were watching the end of the news when Edna got home. Martin stood up and switched off the television.

"How was it then?" Arnold asked as she went over to the fire to dry out her legs and feet.

"Pretty deadly. The speaker wasn't too bad, but there were only about ten there, and the projector wasn't working properly, as usual."

"I don't know why you bother, Mum." Martin flopped back into his chair.

"Someone has to make the tea," she joked. "Margaret Bennett turned up. She tells me she made your acquaintance today."

"Yes. She seems OK. In fact they're not a bad crowd on the whole. Too many women, though. And that Mrs Morley – she's really weird."

"Martin, if I were a churchgoer I'd pin two texts over your bed. One would be 'Judge not' and the other 'Blessed are the meek'."

Arnold laughed.

"He'll grow out of it. He turned to Martin. "But I think you're going to have to learn the hard way, son."

"What's Grace done to upset you?" asked his mother.

"Oh, nothing in particular. She's such a twit, though, prancing about like a great kid at her age." Aware that Edna had known Grace since she was a child, he prodded her for a response, deliberately not mentioning the Zoe incident, and the other characteristics he'd noted in Grace.

"And what age might that be?" Edna smiled. "She's quite a bit younger than I am." She moved away from the fire and sat down beside Arnold on the settee. "And she's had some pretty rough times in her life."

"I shouldn't think she's exactly on the breadline now, though, is she?"

"I'm not talking about money, love. Grace's mother died when she was born and when Harry Allen re-married it wasn't a happy outcome as far as Grace was concerned. She got married herself at seventeen, mainly to get away from her step-mother, but that didn't work out and her husband left her after a year or two. There was a divorce, and she finally married Roger. You know I don't normally gossip, but I have heard they couldn't have any family, much as Grace would have liked children."

"Mmm, well, I asked for that, I suppose." Martin looked somewhat shamefaced, and Arnold said:

"'Jump not to conclusions' might be another one to hang over your bed, eh?"

Martin stretched and stood up.

"I'm off. Thanks – it does help sometimes to listen to a bit of gossip. 'Night, both."

"I wonder what he meant by that, exactly," said Edna.

A few streets away Alan Hancock lay awake.

Over an hour earlier, when they had switched off the light at near to midnight he had thought, exhausted to the point almost of pain: tonight I must surely sleep.

Beside him Laura breathed irregularly, her limbs twitching. He heard his father's rasping snores in the next room.

Outside, the gusty wind bullied the branches of the evergreen in the front garden, causing the light from the street lamp to pitch and roll crazily on the ceiling.

Daylight's images wrestled fretfully with each other to claim his reluctant attention. Eyes closed or open, he saw them, still:

Laura's face, unrecognisably hard as she argued; his father's hands shaking as he struggled to fill his pipe; Kevin Smith's trembling mouth when Alan had flung the mis-spelled, hopelessly inadequate exercise back onto the boy's desk; the startled disbelief of the whole class when he had, for the first time in over thirty years' teaching, bellowed his lost patience at them in fury.

What was happening to him, for God's sake?

Angrily he threw back the blankets and Laura stirred. In a momentary contrite return to the years of accustomed consideration for each other which had characterised their marriage, he edged carefully out of bed so as not to disturb her further.

Downstairs he switched on the gas-fire, reached for a cigarette and slumped into his father's battered old armchair. It was the one incongruous piece of furniture in the neat, tastefully modern room.

Drained as he felt mentally, physically, emotionally, the treadmill of his need to resolve some part of this god-awful situation drove his thoughts on. The mild anaesthetic of the cigarette alleviated slightly the feelings of alarm which had become unpleasantly familiar of late. His customary analytical approach to problems, of whatever nature, began to surface.

He rehearsed what Laura had said a few hours earlier, and told himself that she could not have meant a word of it. Laura, stable, reliable, compassionate and – still, after thirty years – beloved Laura, had spoken quite determinedly of leaving; of being unable to carry on without breaking, if his father stayed. The nicotine was powerless now against the renewed swirl of panic in his guts as he confronted this well-nigh unimaginable prospect.

Two years of trying desperately, and with kindness, to assimilate into their life the bitter, demanding, egocentric stranger who had once been his father had changed them both. Until his wife's death had catapulted George Hancock into their home, Alan and Laura had been a unit. Now, that unit was shattered into sharp, spiteful fragments of tension, disagreement and discord. Even the kids, on their infrequent flights back into their old nest from busy and purposeful worlds, had noticed the change, and left again with puzzled sadness in their eyes.

Little wonder that his teaching, along with himself, seemed to be disintegrating.

Nothing solved, no nearer peace, he hauled himself back to bed and cat-napped away the remainder of the wild dark hours.

Towards dawn the gale blew itself out and the morning offered a rainy, bleak autumn world.

Laura, shoulders held rigid as she prepared breakfast, turned to him briefly.

"I've left a list on the shelf there. You can reach me at Joan's if I've forgotten anything. There's plenty of food to last until you can get out on Saturday. I'll leave before you come in at teatime. Tell Dad anything you like, but not that I'm coming back."

The shuffling of his father's slippered feet on the wood-block floor of the hall sent a blade of screaming resentment slicing through Alan's brain. He was gripping the table edge as George pushed open the kitchen door, slamming it back, as every time, onto the side of the cupboards. Alan's knuckles whitened.

George looked at each of them, his eyes darts of suspicion.

"Cat got yer tongues?" he growled as neither of them spoke. He pointed to his side-plate. "Yer can chuck that toast out for a start. Yer know me teeth wunna tek it, I've towd ye time an' agen."

Laura turned and left the kitchen.

Alan heard the bedroom door close sharply.

"Dad..." his voice cracked. He tried again:

"Laura's going to stay with her sister for a bit. It'll be just you and me for a few days. I've got to get off for school in a minute, but I'll phone at lunchtime to see you're OK, and I'll be in about five tonight.

"What's up then, eh? She can't just off and leave me on me own all day. An' you know I can't 'ear that well on t'phone, so you needn't bother ringing. An dunna expect owt ready at teatime. Yer know 'er ladyship dunna like me messin' about in 'er kitchen."

Alan looked at the clock.

"I'll have to go, Dad. Be careful won't you, and make sure you don't drop any lighted matches."

"I may be eighty-two, but I'm non daft."

His father slurped at his cup of tea.

Alan went upstairs.

The bedroom door was locked.

Chapter 5

The weather had changed again, and an Indian summer glowingly eased out the last days of October. When Margaret arrived at the small house just outside Sheffield Eva Bennett was on her knees in the front garden. She heard the click of the gate and stood up.

She really doesn't look seventy-one, Margaret thought, as she watched her mother walk slowly but steadily towards her.

"Hullo, Mother. Busy as ever?"

"Just getting the last of the bulbs in. I'm a bit late with them this year but I expect they'll survive." She gathered up the kneeling pad and trowel, and giving a final gentle pat to the soil, went on: "I always find it such a comforting idea, in the depths of winter, that there's all that colour and scent nestling in the ground, waiting to come up and cheer us in the spring."

They went indoors and almost before Margaret had had time to take off her jacket and drop her holdall there was coffee on the table by the window. She sat down.

"Bless you – just what I need. You look well, Mother."

"More than I can say for you, love. You look worn out. Anything wrong?"

"No, no. It's been a bit hectic this last week, that's all. Not that it ever seems anything else these days. I'm all right though, really. And a couple of days here with you will work wonders – it always does."

"You're not regretting taking this job at – what's it called – Moortop, are you?"

"Gracious no, I'm not sorry at all. For one thing it's good to be so much nearer here, and to feel I can pop over more often to see you. It's certainly harder work than the London job, and more responsibility – though I don't mind that. But like all nursing jobs, there are times when you wish you could do more, specially for some of our poor old dears."

She sipped at her coffee.

"What's your Matron like? Do you get on?"

"Ah, now you've really asked me something. I'm in a bit of a spot where Miss Gifford's concerned. I can't be sure yet how much it's known round the hospital, but she's obviously over fond of the bottle."

"Oh dear me. Are you sure?"

"No doubt at all. There've been two or three times since I've been there when she's been what's politely called "indisposed", and I've had to take over. I gather it's been like that for quite a time, but no-one so far has given the slightest hint that they know what's really the matter."

"Is that what you meant when you said more responsibility?"

"That's part of it, certainly. It's tricky deciding at what point professional loyalty has to come before feelings for a colleague with problems. And in many ways she's not a bad old stick – very much of the old school, though. One thing's for sure, if it ever comes to a time when it interferes with the care for the patients, then I shan't have any choice"

"I don't envy you, dear. What a horrid position to be in – and I suppose there's no-one you can talk it over with, is there?"

"So far I've not even thought of doing that, but I can't think of anyone, no. Still, that's my problem – don't let's spoil the weekend discussing Moortop. It's good to get a break from it. What's your news?"

As the two women prepared lunch, Eva talked contentedly of her various activities, Margaret wondering afresh at her mother's undiminished interest in life, and her quiet enthusiasms.

"I've had a letter from Jane," she said as they laid the table. "She's thinking of selling up and going into a home –

somewhere in Lincolnshire, I believe."

"I hope she's not making a mistake," said Margaret. "I can't imagine Aunt Jane anywhere but in Cliff House."

"She's getting on, you know, like me, and it's a big place for her to keep up just for herself. Besides, I think she's found it more difficult than some do to come to terms with Arthur's death. They'd been married for nearly fifty years, after all."

"I really must go and see her now that I'm nearer. That's one good thing she'll get if she's in a home, the company. She's always been the spark of your side of the family, hasn't she?

Eva laughed.

"Yes. You could always be sure, even when we were children, that if there was a scrape to get into, Jane would be there first – and she kept that up for most of her life. I don't think even I know the half of it. There was more than one scandal when they were in India, if some of her tales are to be believed."

They spent the afternoon tidying up the garden together, each savouring in her own way the support of their quiet companionship which needed no expression in words. When the light failed they went indoors again and Eva put a match to the fire. After tea they sat in the semi-darkness.

"What you were saying about Aunt Jane," said Margaret. "If only it were possible in some magic way to have some kind of a record of everybody's life – not just the famous ones, but ordinary people – before they die and take all the details with them."

Eva waited, sensing that her daughter had not yet reached the kernel of her idea.

"Do you think we'd understand ourselves and each other better then, or not? I mean, I wish I could get at what really happens when people get old – why so many get that withdrawn look as though they weren't here any more –

and why others seem to be still whole, all of a piece, not resenting age."

"Isn't it because of what kind of a life we've led?" asked Eva.

"I used to think that, but now I don't. It doesn't add up, that theory. Over the years I've seen too many who really haven't had a bad deal, and yet there's that kind of mask on their faces – fear, or resignation, I don't know. And then some hang on and on, bitter and angry, seeming to hate their lot, yet often it's the quiet, contented ones who slip away when you'd think they had so much going for them. We had one only this last week. She was only in for a few hours. She'd had a fall, but nothing broken, and she seemed to be all set for going home again after a few days' rest. Then she just went in the night. Why?"

"I don't suppose we're meant to know the answers to that kind of question," said Eva. "I know you aren't a believer in the way I am, but I'm sure it's possible to ask too many questions."

"You sound a bit like Doctor Rayner." Margaret gave an impatient poke at the fire, sending a criss-crossing haze of sparks into the chimney. "I was talking to him about this the other day and he more or less ticked me off – quite courteously, of course – telling me to concentrate on what I'm supposed to be good at – making what life the patients have got left a bit easier for them, not to get metaphysical, he said! But understanding what's happening inside people is surely part of that?" She paused. "You know, Mum, I still miss Brian, even after all these years. He'd have known what I was talking about, I'm sure, and in a way there's a sort of connection in my mind between the waste of all those young men's lives in the war and the waste at the other end of life for all the thousands who are written off just because they're old. Shoved into a kind of mental waiting room, knowing their train is never going to arrive."

"If it helps, Meg, I don't feel written off..."

Margaret broke in.

"I know you don't. That's just it. Why don't you? And what is it that makes that important difference between people like you, and the others who get cantankerous, or grow a mask, a sort of ghost-look?"

"Do you think it's because most people have no choice but to take what life throws at them, good and bad, and according to the way we're made we either accept with a good grace and learn to make the best of things, or we don't, and those that don't probably gradually grow more bitter and resentful as the years go by. Then again, when you know there's not a lot more time to stand and be Aunt Sallies for whatever's left to be thrown at you, I suspect something else may happen. Lots of old people give in then and say Right, I'm out of it all now. It's just a matter of waiting."

"For the train that won't come?"

"Maybe. But while they wait, some perhaps look both backwards and forwards, wondering what it was all for, bewildered at the idea of going out like a light without knowing why they've burned up all that oxygen for so many years. Some are afraid, that's for sure, but I think most are just pre-occupied with the wondering. Could that explain your ghost-mask?"

She got up and drew the curtains, switching on a small sidelight.

"Meg, love, we'll talk more about this if you want to another time, but I'm a bit tired and I'm getting up for early service tomorrow."

"Oh Mother, I'm sorry. I didn't mean to go on about it. But I do value what you think, you know, and it does help to talk to you. You go on up – I won't be long. Have a good night – I'll bring you a cup of tea in bed in the morning."

She leaned back in her chair as her mother went out. She could hear in the distance the faint drone of the city's night wakefulness but here, in the familiar room, quietness wrapped her round with peace. She began to hope that there might actually be answers to some of the questions she was asking herself. One thing was becoming clearer to her, the importance of distinguishing between knowledge and wisdom – the one treacherously liable to lead to arrogance, the other expanding the capacity for compassion and true understanding.

Chapter 6

Colin had to knock twice on Martin's bedroom door before getting a response.

"Down in a minute." Then Martin looked up from his books as the door opened.

"Oh, Colin, hullo. Sorry – I thought it was Mum to tell me the meal was ready."

"All right to come in for a minute? Your mother said to come straight up."

"Yes, you're OK. Come on in and sit down. What news?"

"I got a letter this morning – after that interview last week. I told you it was a doddle compared with those we had for University. They've accepted me, anyway."

"Great. Tell me more."

Colin rubbed his hands and bounced on to the bed. Martin pushed his worktable to one side, aware of relief and enthusiasm beneath his friend's casual manner.

"What do you want to know? There were about twenty of us there, and they've taken on eight, including me. As from the first of January I shall, to quote the Clodge, be joining the worthy ranks of the British working force. Salt of the earth, me!"

He stood up, drooped his shoulders and touched his forelock.

"Buffool." Martin pushed him back onto the bed. In common with their circle at Barford High, he and Colin had developed a vocabulary largely unintelligible to anyone but themselves. Frank Lodge, a geography and RI master with pretensions to liberal attitudes, had epitomised for many of his pupils the pseudo values they so mistrusted. Dubbed "The Clodge", he had become a useful shorthand symbol when they wanted to express irony.

"What's the job really about, though?"

"Trainee manager. Two years to learn the trade and how to handle men. They didn't say anything about handling women, now that I come to think about it. Ah well, you can't have it all ways I suppose."

"None of the drag of grant applications for you now, eh?"

"The money's the best bit. Not too fantastic the first year, but you get lodging allowance and quite reasonable pay for a beginner. Then after that it's easy all the way. At the end of two years I reckon I can have enough saved to get hitched and I think that's going to be all right with Maureen. We don't have to wait two years for everything, though, do we? – nudge, nudge."

"Well, good for you. If that's what you really want."

"What else? Why don't you think about something like it yourself? D'you really want to go on living on the breadline for all those years, just to end up with letters after your name?"

"You know there's more to it than that, Col. I'm still keen on doing medicine – more than ever now, in fact. And you don't exactly starve on a grant, you know. Nor have I any intention of getting married at the moment, so I've only myself to think about. Still, I really am glad you're fixed up. It means curtains for the Jazz Group, for sure, and I shall miss you, you great idiot. It'll never be the same around here once you've gone."

Colin struck a pose, and fluttered his eyelids.

"Darling, I didn't know you cared."

They both giggled, and then Colin asked:

"What's Moortop like, then? Maureen's gran was admitted the other day – stroke or something. She's quite done about it – so many people have told her that once you go Up the Hill you don't often come down again."

"I've not been there long enough to judge, really. In any case, working in the office you don't see all that much of the patients." Martin paused. "But for what it is, it seems

a pretty OK place. A lot less depressing than I expected, too
– and you can tell Maureen it's not true that patients never
get out once they're in. Quite a few of them do get home
again."

"How much longer have you got there?" asked Colin.

"Not sure. I shouldn't think it'll be much after
Christmas. The bloke whose job I'm doing seems to be
getting better, and once he comes back I'll be on the dole
again. Still, more time for this –" He gestured towards his
books. "I'm determined not to fluff my A levels again."

"There speaks the dedicated swot. I still think you're
a fool, Brookes, but I know I'm not likely to change your
mind. What time at the George tonight, then – and it's my
treat. Eightish?"

"Right, I'll be there – and thanks."

"See you, kid." He slapped his friend's shoulder and
Martin heard his noisy shout to Edna as he let himself out
of the front door. He turned back to his textbooks. Only a
few short months ago he and Colin and other friends had
talked about the world being their oyster. His particular
pearl sometimes seemed pretty small, and he had to look
hard to see its gleam.

The bus stop in Barford Market Place was exposed
and draughty and the huddle of passengers waiting for the
5.30 Delton bus drew closer together as though to share
their discomfort. But Maureen Spendlove remained slightly
apart from the others, at the back of the queue. When the
bus finally appeared it was already nearly full and taking
the last seat available she found herself next to Mrs
Turnbull.

"Hello Maureen, me duck." The older woman moved
a loaded shopping bag onto her lap from the seat beside
her.

"Looks as if winter's coming early, doesn't it? And
after all that lovely sunshine last weekend, too."

Maureen answered as briefly as courtesy allowed. She preferred to occupy her journeys to and from her work in the Barford Town Hall offices by reading rather than exchanging the small talk of chance encounters, but to have opened her book now would be inexcusably rude, so she resigned herself to twenty minutes of mild irritation.

"Sorry to hear about your Grandma, Maureen. How is she?"

"Holding her own at the moment, thank you. I haven't seen her yet, but my parents went again last night and it seems that if she gets through the next few days all right she stands a good chance."

"What happened exactly? I heard your Mum found her."

"That's right. It was last week. She called round on the Thursday as usual, just after breakfast, to collect Gran's pension book and see if she wanted any shopping. Gran had apparently got up and dressed herself and started to make her breakfast, and then had the stroke. She seemed to be unconscious, but the ambulance was very quick once Mother had phoned, and Gran was in Moortop by lunchtime."

"Poor soul." Mrs Turnbull clucked her sympathy. "Such a capable and cheerful old lady, your Gran was. I never heard her grumble. But there, we never know what's coming to us, do we?

Mrs Turnbull's assumptive use of the past tense jarred, and Maureen didn't answer.

Undeterred, Mrs Turnbull went on:

"Well, she's in the best place. Whatever can be done for her, they'll do Up the Hill. Ever so kind they are there. I remember when I went to see old Alice Peabody last year – nothing was too much trouble for them with her. And she was in a very bad way, you know. Been neglecting herself something shocking, she had, towards the end. And look at the way they got old Jock Mumford back on his feet in no time..."

With Mrs Turnbull well launched into her monologue of Delton gossip Maureen felt free to pursue her own thoughts, although the route they took was twisted, confusing as a labyrinth, and clouded in places by guilt. Her closeness to and love for Granny Spendlove had for a long time seemed more significant than her feelings for her parents. She'd have to tell them soon that she was planning to get a flat in Barford. Gran had guessed that she wanted to try living on her own, and they'd talked about how her mother and father would be surprised, hurt. Now Gran couldn't talk at all. It was as if a big hole had opened up in front of her. And where did Colin fit into everything? Did she really want to marry him – had he even meant it seriously when he'd suggested it, knowing that last year she and Martin...

The bus braked suddenly, shooting the passengers forward, and Mrs Turnbull's shopping bag fell. The stream of gossip was effectively dammed whilst Maureen helped her to retrieve apples, packets of tea and tubes of Smarties from under the seat in front, as the bus resumed its journey.

"Thanks ever so, duck." Mrs Turnbull sat back again, red in the face, patting her hat straight and hugging the shopping bag tightly to her. "It's a mercy you were here to help, else I don't know what I'd've done. Our Carol and Darren'd never forgive me if I hadn't got their Smarties to give them when I get home. Course, their Mam says I spoil them, but what's a Nana for if it's not to spoil her grandchildren, I always say."

The bus stopped in Delton High Street and Maureen stood up.

"Cheerio, dear," said Mrs Turnbull, whose stop was on the other side of the town. "I've so enjoyed our little talk. Give my best to your Gran when you see her."

"Yes I will. Goodnight."

Later that evening, Maureen set out on her own for the cold walk up to Moortop.

"You'll find Gran very much changed," her father had said, and she wondered as she climbed the lane how she'd cope with this meeting. In fact she was totally unprepared for what she found.

> *The voices – giants' voices; faces, giants' faces, but suddenly getting smaller for no good reason, until they were only pinpricks of sound and light. Hands not her own, some rough, some gentle, taking over everything – moving, washing, feeding. Propelled from darkness to light, from one day to the next, in a haze of vagueness and worry. She talked, sometimes anxiously, sometimes in gratitude, now and then in temper. But no-one heard, no-one even listened. They smiled, they soothed, but she might have been talking in a foreign language. Remote – that was the word; it was all so remote. Perhaps she wasn't actually talking at all? She couldn't hear her own voice. Only strange noises; sometimes "No – no", sometimes a sort of drunken blabber, seeming to come from her mouth, though she hadn't meant it to sound like that.*
>
> *Often there were warm tears on her face, a moisture running down somewhere near her chin. But she wasn't crying, was she?*
>
> *And then Hughlinda came, a single, strange two-bodied figure in trousers and a skirt, and went away without leaving the shopping. Hughlinda sat up on the gas-cooker although she tried and tried to tell him-her to get down. She-he opened the secret drawer in the kitchen cabinet and wiped her chin with the pound notes hidden there for emergencies...*

Gran was propped up in a high-backed chair beside her bed. Her normally neatly styled hair was clean and combed, yet it looked somehow bedraggled. Her dress hung crookedly on her shoulders, so that the useless side of her body was emphasised; there were spots of spilled food on her bodice. In one hand she had gathered a knitted knee-rug into folds on her lap and her legs, thus exposed in wrinkled stockings were stiff, awkwardly-angled excrescences. But it was the sight of her grandmother's face which affected Maureen most profoundly and she had to force herself to bend down to kiss the yellowish cheek.

This was not Granny Spendlove, but some hideously mocking waxwork sitting there. The familiar features were so nearly true that the strange twistedness, the emptiness behind the eyes, the sickly colouring almost persuaded Maureen that she was looking at a cunningly devised counterfeit.

She made an effort at self-control and spoke.

"Hullo then, Gran, what in the world have you been up to?"

At first she wasn't sure whether the old woman had heard. Then the vacant eyes strained at her and the lips seemed to be trying to smile. For a moment Maureen felt that she might be visiting the wrong patient. Bewildered, she took the old woman's hand.

"It's me, Gran. Maureen. Don't you remember?"

A faint noise passed through the slack mouth, and then Flo turned her head away with a strange reptilian movement, the eyes turning urgently towards the end of the ward, as though expecting that relief, wholeness, normality might come in through the swing doors and re-enter her.

This movement was repeated several times during the few minutes that Maureen sat there. She tried to talk normally, to report items of local news, to give the messages from friends who had sent their good wishes. She heard her own voice rising, her words being articulated artificially as though to a deaf mental defective, and dismayed, she checked herself.

A nurse rang a bell at the ward entrance. Despising herself for the sense of relief which flowed through her, Maureen got up, squeezed the limp hand, and left.

She had been home for some time when her parents returned from a rehearsal of the local dramatic society's Christmas pantomime.

"How was Gran, then?" asked her father.

She began to cry. Her mother sat down beside her, saying:

"Don't upset yourself now. Perhaps we shouldn't have let you go on your own for the first time. It was probably too much of a shock for you."

"Rubbish!" Hugh Spendlove's voice was sharp with his own anxiety and unhappiness. "She's nearly twenty – a grown woman! She's always rabbiting on about leading her own life, but when it comes down to facing some of the worries and responsibilities of being an adult, it's a different story."

"I'll go and make us all a cup of something," said Linda.

"No, I'll go Mother." Maureen stood up. "Sorry I made a fool of myself."

When she came back into the sitting-room with the tray, Hugh said more quietly:

'Do you think Gran knew you, then?"

"I don't know. It's as though she's there and yet not there, isn't it? She isn't my Gran any more, that's what's so awful."

Linda said: "It won't always be like that, dear. We met one of the senior people when we were there last night – a Miss Bennett, I think her name is – and she was quite hopeful that Gran will be all right eventually, but we can't rush things."

"What if she doesn't get properly better, though? Supposing she were to end up like some of those other old women in there? It'd be better if she'd died."

"That's enough, Maureen!" The sharp note returned to Hugh's voice. "Just think of Gran, not your own feelings for once. It's up to all of us to do what we can to help her, encourage her to get better..."

"I know, *I know* all that. It's just that I'm afraid that – oh, never mind. Sorry again that I got so upset. If you don't mind, though, I won't come with you tomorrow. Colin's got tickets for the dance at the Town Hall, so I'll give him a ring and tell him I'll go with him after all. Perhaps I'll go and see her on Sunday."

When she had gone out, Hugh turned exasperatedly to his wife.

"What's the matter with that girl? She's always claimed to be so fond of mother, spending hours talking to her and doing things for her, and yet now she's as good as said she wishes this stroke had killed her. I don't understand."

"She's had a shock, seeing your mother like she is. I blame myself for not realising how it might upset her."

"I still don't think she's cause to say what she did. She wants to grow up a bit, as I say, and start thinking more of other people. Doesn't she appreciate how upset we are?"

"Now, Hugh, let it drop. Maureen's not a bad girl on the whole – though I must admit I'm a bit worried about her seeing so much of Colin Wilkinson. I hope it doesn't get too serious – he's a bit of a wild type, I've always thought, and younger than she is, too. Oh, by the way, did you hear what Peggy Rushton was saying tonight about Laura Hancock having left Alan?"

"Good Lord, no. Are you sure?"

"Seems like it. She's apparently gone to her sister's – you know, Joan – she lives across from Peggy on Highcroft Avenue, and she's definitely seen her there all this last week, and the word is she's not going back to Alan."

"You women – talk about unpredictable... I'd have

bet any money that marriage was a permanent fixture if ever there was one. They must be in their fifties, aren't they?"

"Yes, well, there it is. No-one seems to know the reason – I can't imagine Alan being the unfaithful husband somehow – perhaps it's Laura who's gone off the rails."

"Poor old Alan. Doesn't his father live with them now?"

"As far as I know he's still there, yes. Goodness knows how Alan's coping – his Dad must be well over eighty. Whatever Laura was thinking of to walk out on them, I don't know."

On the following evening Alan, grey fatigue clothing him like a second skin, sat listening to Dr Bradshaw imposing upon him a seemingly unlimited sentence of despair.

"Believe me, Alan, if there were anything, anything at all I could do to help I would. But as long as he's got a home with you and is reasonably healthy and mentally OK, I haven't got a single string I can pull. Even for those poor old devils who've no family to call on, some of 'em living in conditions we know are intolerable, there's a waiting list as long as my arm for all the newer homes, even for temporary periods. Unless you're prepared to consider private care..."

Alan snorted.

"On a teacher's salary?"

"No, well. At the moment I can hold out little hope, but if you like I'll put his name down for Moortop. It might be a long wait, though."

"No!" The word spurted from Alan,

He had once gone Up the Hill to visit the shrivelled wreck of an ex-colleague, prematurely senile, sitting hunched in glazed-eyed isolation. He had vowed then that no-one of his should ever be condemned to that. And yet wasn't his father equally isolated now – perhaps more so – in his dissociation from himself and Laura? At least in Moortop there would be others to share his prejudices, his exclusion.

"Alan, I don't want to rush you, but you've seen for yourself how busy the surgery is... Will you let me at least give you something to help you sleep?"

He shook his head and stood up.

"Sorry Peter, I'll get away now. No, no tablets thanks. I don't want to get on that trail. Anyway, if I took anything I'd never hear Dad if he called in the night."

Peter Bradshaw paused. Then:

"No way I can help with Laura and yourself, I suppose? You've only to ask, you know"

Again Alan shook his head.

"No, thanks all the same. I expect we'll work things out somehow. At least we still talk, even if it's only by phone. But I appreciate the offer. 'Night."

The white front door of the modern semi which had always welcomed him now threatened as he inserted his key. Inside he called, as he had done all his married life.

"I'm home," but his voice tonight was pewter coloured.

Crouched over the gas-fire in a haze of cheap tobacco fumes, his father looked up.

"'Ow long d'ye think we can keep this up?" he barked. "Yer mam'd turn in her grave if she knew. 'Alf past six, and no square meal sin' this time yesterday."

"Won't be long, Dad. Soon have the kettle on. You might at least have done that. I told you I'd be a bit late in."

"Yer want to get that woman of your'n back where she belongs, that's all. 'Er place is 'ere, lookin' after us, not gallivantin' with 'er flamin' sister."

Shutting the living-room door gently was a deliberate exercise in control, one of the many he now practised daily, striving with each such act to maintain undamaged his understanding of and closeness to Laura, who had endured this situation almost unalleviated for two years.

Later, he sat with his father through hours of noisy television, trying to shut out both sound and vision.

Hot-water bottle filled, glass of water by his bed, next to the basin he used as a spittoon to relieve his nightly bronchial congestion, his father was finally removed, at least for the next few hours, from Alan's immediate physical consciousness,

Downstairs again he sat staring into the apparent ruin of his life. It couldn't last for ever, this desperately unsatisfactory holding operation. But afterwards...?

What did other people do? All the other thousands who were clinging to the straw of a dream future when the old man, the old woman, would not be there to release the poison of quite irrational guilt? What was the outlook for himself, Laura, all their generation, when they too would reach the waste-land?

It was a denial of one's whole past to acknowledge that there might be any situation so totally untenable, any problem without some solution, and yet here... now...?

He recalled his Deputy Head telling him, at the time of his divorce from Betty, that loneliness even as far as monastic celibacy, was infinitely preferable to the erosion of dignity which could result from the relentless gnawings of incompatibility. That when love and respect went, there was little basis for co-existence.

And yet he, Alan, had loved his father; had respected him for his views, his straightness, his refusal to be downed by a life of drudgery; had appreciated the sacrifices he and Mum had made to give their kids a better chance. They – he and Laura – had had such fine ideas, when Mum died, about providing a supportive easing for his father through his last years. Instead, this descent into a carping, degrading, never-abating state of near hatred. For his own father...

And daily Laura had grown more quiet, clinging to the firm centre of her self for support, but increasingly unable to sustain the burden of his own need for relief lest she broke down completely, bringing down all three of them into total darkness.

Now he saw the wisdom of her going. Hold on to that – a positive among so many negatives.

Nearly midnight. He made a token attempt to tidy the living-room. Saturday tomorrow. Perhaps when he'd done the washing and the shopping and cleaned through, he'd go over and see Laura.

Chapter 7

The annals of the monotonous routines which were the daily lot of most residents in The House did contain sporadic punctuation marks: the commas of new arrivals; the full-stops of sudden death, the exclamation marks of occasional physical fights.

There were also under-scorings, occasioned by The Events. In addition to celebrations at Easter and Christmas, and the appropriate marking – by tea-parties or prayers – of Royal Weddings and Births or State Funerals, attempts were made to relieve the residents' tedium with concerts, outings and other diversions.

Miss Gifford had, early in her tenure, tried to convince her staff of the value of such efforts in "stimulating the responses" and "broadening the horizons" of their charges. Although it had been noticed that her personal enthusiasm had waned considerably of late, the reflex reactions she had once activated continued now without her prompting.

Today's Event was to be the concert that evening, given – as it was every year during the last week of November – by a local choir calling themselves the Delton Songbirds.

Today, too, Robert North, ex-concert party singer, one-time Guildhall student, had a visitor. This was something so unusual that several of his fellow-residents made no attempt to hide their curiosity. Eddie even risked a comment:

"Crafty owd devil, Bob. Y'never towd us you 'ad a lady friend."

Miss Frost, carrying a metal chair into the dayroom, hushed Eddie sharply and he chortled, wheezing, and screwing up his pasty stubbled features. He banged his stick on the floor to applaud himself.

The visitor sat down and arranged her over-made-up face into what she believed was a cheerful and interested expression. The visit had come about because Mrs Blake had remarked that it might cheer Robert up to meet one of the singers and have a chat, "Seeing as how he used to do a bit of singing himself, like," she'd said.

As attendant in charge, Harriet preferred to be the instigator of any ideas concerning the residents, but even a casual observer might have noticed that her imagination could not be called fertile. In any case she believed that if these people ended up in Moortop it was probably their own fault; if they were being fed, clothed and kept as clean as possible they couldn't and shouldn't expect much else. However, when Elsie Blake had made the suggestion about Robert, she'd taken it up. Although Matron Gifford no longer seemed interested enough for it to be worth trying to impress her, Harriet thought she might gain a plus point with Miss Bennett, who seemed increasingly to be the one to keep in with. So it was that when Hilda Harris, the organiser of the Songbirds, arrived to make the final arrangements for the concert, Harriet told her about Robert.

"He used to be in the entertainment world, went round singing at concerts for the troops during the war, that sort of thing." (Harriet had briefed herself during the morning from Robert's notes.) "I suppose after the war he'd be too old to start again seriously, and then he took to drink. He's only been here a few months – came to us from lodgings in Barford. He's not that old, of course, in his mid-sixties, but he looks more. He's suffering from depression. Doesn't say very much, but we thought perhaps you could get him to open up a bit."

Hilda, full of sentimental goodwill, and flattered by the request, now set about playing the role of amateur therapist with enthusiasm.

"Now then Robert – I can call you Robert, can't I?"

She simpered, touching her hair. "Miss Frost tells me you and I have a lot in common."

Robert sat silent. He had been a handsome man in his time, and even now the thick white hair brushed back over his head gave him a look of distinction. Alcohol had coloured his complexion unnaturally and there was defeat in his eyes, but there was still an air of urbanity about him.

Hilda tried again.

"I hope we've got at least one of your favourite numbers in our programme tonight. What sort of field was your speciality?"

Still Robert said nothing, but now he did look at her.

Stupid bitch he thought. Stupid brainless bitch. Sitting there thinking she's doing me some kind of a favour. I could tell her tales that'd make those silly false eyelashes drop off. All that face-powder and that frizzy black hair – if that's not a wig I'm a Dutchman. Must be sixty if she's a day. And that scent – same cheap bloody stuff that Mamie used to drench herself with in the days of the old Thirties Follies.

The contempt in his thoughts showed in his eyes, but Hilda pressed on, either not seeing or choosing to ignore it.

"We shall be doing 'All in the April Evening' and 'The Bells of Saint Mary's' – they always go down well," she chattered. "I'm sure you know those. And then we always have one or two choruses for you all to join in at the end."

Robert gave a grunt and picked up a newspaper from the floor beside his chair.

Hilda stood up, smiling on determinedly but failing to conceal a tremor of what might have been rage, embarrassment, even fear.

"See you tonight then, Robert. And I shall be listening for your contribution when we start the community singing."

Eddie's delighted whoop followed her progress to the door.

Harriet was in the hall with the electrician, who was checking the stage lighting.

"I didn't have much success, I'm afraid," Hilda told her. "He's very down, isn't he? P'raps he'll cheer up a bit when we get going tonight. We'll be here about half-past six, then, for a seven o'clock start, if that's all right?"

She picked up a tattered notebook and a pile of music from the piano stool and hurried out to her own hummed version of "Alice Blue Gown".

When Martin arrived to help at the concert, the hall was filling with wheelchairs carrying patients brought over from the wards. He joined the other staff and a few visitors who were pushing the chairs into a close-packed series of semi-circles facing the stage. Behind them were rows of wooden chairs where a few residents were already in their places, and more were wandering in through the French doors in the side of the hall in ones and twos. Martin raised his hand in greeting to Joe and Eddie and spoke to Robert. He had come to know several of the men over the past weeks. Few of the audience looked eager. Some were bewildered, patently uncertain why they were there at all. Others grumbled audibly, muttering that they'd rather be watching the telly.

Making her way between the rows and smiling brightly, Matron Gifford tucked in a rug here, adjusted a tie there. Miss Bennett was doing her best under difficulties to ensure that a clear gangway was being left down the middle of the rows for emergencies.

At last it seemed that everyone was assembled, and Miss Gifford went round to the rear of the stage; some of the lights in the hall went off and the noise from the audience was augmented by stumbles, chair-scraping and throat-clearing from behind the curtains. As these were drawn back and a repeated thumping chord was struck on the piano there was a disturbance in the body of the hall.

Hilda Harris's opening remarks were lost in the

noise of wheelchairs being moved around to allow one near the back to be pushed out again by a red-faced young nurse. Martin watched, amused, as other staff hastily moved their charges' chairs to cover up a slowly spreading pool on the polished floor.

The concert began.

Between each item, diamante jewellery flashing on her oversized bust and sequins shimmering on her long purple dress, Hilda made her announcements, her voice becoming ever more shrill in her attempt to cut some kind of a swathe through the thick atmosphere of indifference which was almost tangible in the hall. Martin felt almost sorry for her, even though her amateur artiness made him squirm.

As each soloist or small group of singers awkwardly clambered through the main chorus on the overcrowded platform to perform an item from the front of the stage, the restiveness in the audience expressed itself in wails, coughs and shouts. When the songs happened to be familiar, one or two joined in with pathetic croakings.

Martin was suddenly startled out of his growing embarrassment as Robert, who had been sitting beside him, stood up, his chair clattering over backwards to the floor. The choir had embarked on a flat, soulful rendering of "Going Home", which they considered the highlight of their repertoire, particularly in a programme for senior citizens.

"That's not a bloody choral song you idiots," Robert yelled. "It's the New World Symphony and should stay that way."

Martin tried to quieten him, without success. Harriet Frost and a male attendant hurried across and each took one of Robert's arms, firmly turning him towards the door. He continued to shout as he was propelled out of the hall

"Just because I ended up as a third-rate flop myself, it doesn't mean I don't know about music. Call yourselves

Songbirds – braying donkeys, more like..."

The choir sang on but nobody was listening any more, and no-one joined in the community singing which brought the concert to a premature end. Miss Gifford and Harriet Frost tried to pacify the weeping Hilda with cups of watery coffee, and the other members of the choir assured anyone who would listen that they quite understood, were certain most of the old folk had enjoyed the evening, that of course they'd be delighted to come again next year...

Martin, as he took his share of clearing the hall, pondered on Robert's outburst and its probable roots in the man's frustration and unfulfilled ambitions. Quiet eventually settled over The House and Robert, tranquillised now and sleeping soundly, dreamed of the début that had never happened, when he appeared as one of the soloists in a Royal Albert Hall performance of Messiah.

On the Monday morning following the concert the staff in the office learned that Tom Cresswell, their injured colleague, would shortly be returning and that Martin would be going in a couple of weeks. As he was leaving the Hospital Secretary's room Martin asked Mr Barraclough if he might continue to come to Moortop occasionally to visit some of the patients and residents.

"I see no reason why not, but you'd better have a word with Miss Gifford – that side of things is more Matron's province than mine."

He waited in the draughty hallway. Matron had arranged to see him at two o'clock and it was already a quarter past. There had been no answer to his knocks and the door was locked. He was about to turn away when Margaret Bennett hurried in through the outer door, appearing unusually flustered.

"Hallo Martin. Miss Gifford's apologies – she's not feeling too well and she's asked me to see you. Come in."

She unlocked the door.

"Do sit down. What can we do for you?" He explained that he would shortly be leaving and repeated the request he had made to Mr Barraclough.

"Of course we'd be delighted to see you any time, Martin, and I'm sure it'll be a real tonic for anyone you visit. They may not be able to express it, but it means a lot to many of them to feel somebody's interested enough to maintain a relationship with them."

"But I really enjoy talking to them, hearing about their past, finding out what they think and how they feel about life."

Margaret nodded.

"I know just what you mean – although it's not often a young man like you has that sort of interest in old people. I know a lot of youngsters have a special feeling, say, for one particular grandparent but they don't usually have much time for the old in general."

"I didn't think I had until I came here."

He saw that she was waiting for him to say more, and he began to talk, finding that for the first time he was able to put into words some of the ideas and questions generated by his experience in Moortop, and that Margaret not only understood but was able to expand and illuminate.

The clock in the old bell tower struck three, and Martin stood up.

"I'm sorry – I've taken up too much of your time."

"No, that's quite all right Martin. I'm glad we've talked. If you'll remind me before you leave, I'll lend you a couple of books and there's no hurry to let me have them back. I'm sure that when you get to Medical School there'll be plenty of people ready to try to knock your idealism out of you. And some of the things you'll encounter in training will test it even further. I'd like to think that you'll be one of the few who get through to the other end with some of it still intact."

She lifted her hands in a shrug, and smiled.

"There I go – I do *try* not to preach, but I'm afraid I do go on a bit when it's something I feel strongly about. The best of luck, anyway, and I'd like to know how you make out eventually."

Difficult, she thought as he went out, for a lad like that to keep his principles and yet not turn into a prig. She hoped that wouldn't happen, not that he'd compromise. Was she herself compromising, in this situation with Irene Gifford? It couldn't be covered up much longer – she'd been pretty near incoherent when Margaret had left her in the flat an hour ago. She'd better pop back and make sure Irene was at least safe before she completed the afternoon duties. Although nursing had inured her to physical unpleasantness of all kinds, she'd been repelled when she'd found Irene being sick that lunchtime.

"Must have been that curry we had last night," she'd said, giggling as she wiped her mouth, "I won't have any lunch – just a little something to quench my thirst..."

She was asleep when Margaret looked in now, the flush on her cheeks the only sign that she was anything other than "slightly indisposed".

Grace, never needing an excuse for a celebration, happily seized on the occasion of Martin's departure and Tom Cresswell's imminent return, together with the approach of Christmas, to organise an extra office party.

Two or three months ago, Martin would have found her enthusiasm embarrassing. Now he was only faintly uncomfortable. His first impressions of Grace had changed radically and he'd acknowledged to himself that she was the one person on Moortop's staff who had most influenced his emotional attitudes towards old people.

Intellectually he had absorbed ideas and knowledge from books, from observation, from conversations with people like Margaret Bennett. But with Grace he had established an empathy which somehow enhanced his encounters with the patients and residents. His relationship with her was confined to the context of the job. He had never visited her home, nor she his. They spoke little of matters other than Moortop. Yet he knew that he was one of the very few people to whom her sensitivity had been revealed, who had spotted the cracks in her brittle shell. Having had no reason to exploit that fact, he had been given her trust and he was able to see the true caring which underlay her apparent shallowness. He felt he was beginning to grow up.

The party – a relatively quiet gathering – took place after the office had closed on Martin's last day. Grace and Beryl had prepared a modest buffet with a couple of bottles of wine. Martin managed to acquit himself without revealing how ill-at-ease he normally felt in such circumstances. His temporary colleagues presented him with a fountain-pen and when it was all over and he was collecting together his personal belongings, Grace approached him. She pressed a small gift into his hands, saying

"This is just from me. All the best, lad. And give a thought to Zoe Trimmer now and then, eh?"

Chapter 8

Darkness was the best and the worst time. With nothing to see there was less "out there" to try to work out. But then, with nothing visible to puzzle about, the questions inside took over: the wheres, and hows, the whats and whens. And she was totally, utterly alone.

Gradually, though, very gradually, the haze, the queernesses, the absurdities began to disappear. It seemed that there was a routine. Apart from odd, short dark periods during the daylight, when she supposed she nodded off, night and day became separated, as did Hugh-Linda. She learned to recognise which hands would be rough and which gentle, and the sizes of faces were more regular. Only some voices continued to boom and bellow. Others were soothing and kind. One of these only came occasionally, but there was one which was regular, and a green overall, as its wearer swept and wiped, dusted and stacked pots, began to point the way back to normality. Many, many times that period of strange isolation was made just bearable by the presence of the soft voice and the green overall, whose owner never passed by her bed or chair without pausing for a word, a touch.

She realised that food came to her mostly when she was just becoming aware of hunger; that she was taken to the lavatory when she began to feel the discomfort of a full bladder. Then the days became ordered into the familiar pattern of morning, afternoon and evening. One never-to-be-forgotten Friday, Flo recognised the face above the green overall as belonging to Norah Goodwin, who lived across the road from her in Station Street. The links with real life were strengthening.

Still no-one seemed to understand the way she talked inside herself with nothing coming out right, and then she wept with frustration. But slowly, slowly she felt a kind of balance being restored, a tiny glimmer of hope that she wouldn't always be so helpless. She seized eagerly on each tiny achievement and her recovery began.

But where had Maureen gone? Vaguely she recalled her granddaughter's visits, three times, or was it four she'd been? Long, long ago, and now each time she tried to say "Maureen?" to Hugh or Linda, they too were vague.

A week or two before Christmas Maureen and Colin were walking home from a folk concert at the George. It was clear and cold, and the freshness of the night air was welcome after the fug of the pub.

"I'm not promising to write very often you know," said Colin as they reached Limes Avenue. "I never was much good at putting my feelings on paper. But you let me have your phone number when you get into the flat and I'll ring you, OK?"

"Perhaps it's better if neither of us makes too many promises at this stage." Maureen was evasive. "You're sure to find things very different when you get away from here, specially in the South – I bet it won't be like Delton."

"You're not warning me off, are you? The way I feel about you and us – that won't change."

"Let's just leave it, shall we? You'll be home for weekends sometimes, won't you? Let's wait and see how it is..."

"Sure I'm coming back, as often as I can, but I'm not saying it'll be to go home every time. I was hoping the flat – well, you know..."

"Yes, I know. I'm just not sure how it's going to work out. I'm not exactly warning you off, no; just let's wait and see."

"All right, if that's how you want it. But I'm not

easily put off when I want something either, and I do – you."

They had reached her house.

"Blast" she said as they stood at the gate. "The front room light's on. That means they're waiting up. It's like I'm still fourteen, the way they sit up until I'm in. I just can't wait to get into a place of my own."

"Right on, girl! Then I shan't have to kiss you goodnight outside, shall I?"

He felt triumphant as she returned his embrace with a passion which negated what she had said earlier. When she finally broke away and let herself into the house, he walked back along the avenue whistling.

The row erupted as soon as she got indoors.

"Was that Colin Wilkinson with you?" Linda asked, putting down the magazine she was pretending to read.

"And if it was?" Maureen's tone was as icy as her mother's.

"That's no way to answer a civil question." Hugh joined the battle.

"Look, I'm nearly twenty. I think it's my business, and mine alone, who I choose to associate with, and yes, it was Colin."

"I suppose you've been to the George again? I'm surprised you let yourself be seen there after that drugs raid the other week. I wouldn't put it past young Colin to be mixed up in all that."

"That's just typical of you two. Never mind the truth, so long as you're seen to be respectable. I happen to know that Colin wouldn't touch the stuff – any more than I would. We're not all users in our generation, you know."

"Well, I'm glad to hear it. But that isn't why we've stayed up. We've been to see Gran again tonight and she really seems to have turned the corner. In fact it looks as though she'll be out after Christmas."

Shaken, Maureen sat down without taking off her

coat.

"Where will she go? Surely she's not well enough to look after herself yet, is she?"

"Oh no, not for some time. Obviously she'd have to come here." Hugh nodded as Linda went on. "Dad and I have talked it over. We can make up a bed down here for her for the time being, until she can manage the stairs better. Mind you, we've not decided anything definitely until we've discussed it with you. This is your home too, even though you do sometimes treat it like a hotel. It'd mean adjustments all round for all of us."

Maureen drew a deep breath.

"Well, in that case, now seems as good a time as any to broach another subject then. Since you've mentioned changes, I might as well tell you that I've managed to find a flat in Barford and I shall be moving out in the New Year."

Linda gasped. Hugh thumped the arms of his chair.

"When did this idea start? You've never said a word before."

"I've been thinking about it for some time, and now it seems the sooner the better. If Gran comes here it'll be easier for you if I'm not around.

"What in the world d'you mean, girl, easier? I'd imagined you'd be able to help your mother with the extra work it's bound to cause, not walk out and leave it all to her. Besides, you've never made any secret of the fact that you seem to think more of your Gran than you do of us most of the time. What's got into you?"

"Let's face facts for once, shall we Dad? Though you might not like doing that. Gran, for a start – yes, I have got on well with her in the past. She always meant something special to me and she always understood me better than anyone. She even seemed to understand why sometimes I've found you two hard to live with."

"That's a dreadful thing to say about your own parents, Maureen. Haven't we always done our best for you?" Linda said.

"I'm sure you have, and I'm not denying it. But I see such a lot of things differently from the way you do – and so did Gran. Oh, she'd have cut out her tongue sooner than be disloyal about you directly, but we both knew without having to say anything."

"What sort of things? I'm sure I don't know what you mean." Linda's voice, too, was abrasive now.

"If you don't know, there's not a lot of point in cataloguing it all."

"Now come on, Maureen, you don't get out of it that easily," said Hugh. "You've more or less made an accusation there of some sort, so you'd better either back it up or take it back."

"All right then. Politics for one thing – we're poles apart there. The sort of books we read. And bothering what the neighbours think. And keeping up with the Jones's – oh, a whole host of things – we've rowed enough about them over the years, heaven knows. You're not going to change now – and why should you? – and certainly I shan't, so surely it's better if I go."

"And where does Gran come in all this, then? How do you square the marvellous closeness to her that you claim to have, with the fact that you've hardly been near Moortop since she was taken ill? And now you're skiving out of being around to help look after her. Have you any idea what it's been like for us – for me, to see my own mother at death's door? And now she's getting better you don't want to know. I grant you she's changed a bit, isn't quite as quick on the uptake as she used to be, but she's no fool, you know. She's noticed how you've kept away and since she got her speech back a bit she's never failed, not once, to ask about you. Never says 'Why doesn't Maureen come', mind you. But we've been on the defensive every time, had to make excuse after excuse for you. I just don't understand."

"No, I know you don't and that's part of the whole trouble." Maureen spoke more quietly now. "It's just because I was so close to Gran that I can't face pretending to myself, much less to her, that things are still the same as they were before. Oh, she can perhaps shuffle about now with a walking aid, and talk about what she had for lunch, or what the doctor said yesterday. But the Flo Spendlove I knew and loved won't ever go back to 39 Station Street and be able to talk and laugh and cry about all the important things in life. And yes, it may be weak and selfish of me, but at least I'm admitting that I'm not strong enough to act a lie with her."

Linda started to cry. Hugh got up and stood in front of the fire, hands in pockets.

"I hope you're well satisfied, miss, now you've told us what you think of us, and reduced your mother to tears."

"I'm sorry. I didn't want to hurt either of you – I've just tried to be honest. Perhaps we'll get on better when I'm not actually living here – in a funny sort of way I suppose it's because I think it may help to preserve what I feel deep down about you, and Gran, that I feel it's best if I go. I'll come over any time you want help looking after Gran and if she needs someone to be here while you go out, of course I'll come if I can."

There was a long silence.

"Oh, we wouldn't want to put you to any inconvenience." Hugh's sarcasm set Linda weeping afresh. "In fact, you'd perhaps better clear out before Christmas. Your mother and I will be spending most of the time at the hospital anyway – we wouldn't want to think of Gran being on her own up there. P'raps that says something about who really cares for her."

In the solitude of her bedroom, Maureen sobbed herself to sleep.

Alan couldn't remember a less festive Christmas. Even in his childhood, when semi-poverty had laid a drab pall over their home for much of the year, somehow his parents had managed to ensure that for one day in December they could all eat and drink their fill, and be carefree, and enjoy being warm and expansive in body as well as spirit. And he and Laura, by no means well-off in their early days of marriage, had been conventional in this if not in some other respects, and had celebrated Christmas in the same way as long as their own children still lived at home.

He recalled that even last year, with the youngsters visiting, despite his father's gradual decline the old man had seemed to make an effort to suppress the bitterness and hostility which had become his norm, and to respond to their attempts to create the "peace and goodwill" atmosphere.

A week previously Laura had finally relented and returned home, and together they worked towards a period of truce, though postponing the question of the rebuilding of their relationship. Then, on the day before Christmas Eve, George had refused to get up. Complaining that his legs wouldn't support him, but refusing to sanction their calling in Doctor Bradshaw, he stayed in bed. Together they took up his cards and the family presents on Christmas morning but he showed no interest in them, nor in the meals which Laura painstakingly prepared as though everything were normal.

By the evening of Christmas Day, Alan was worried enough to say:

"Shall I ring Peter and ask him to pop over? I'm sure he wouldn't mind, Christmas or not"

"You heard what your father said yesterday," answered Laura. "I'll bet he wouldn't co-operate, even if Peter did come. I wouldn't put it past him to get up and dress, and claim there was nothing wrong with him. Think how we'd feel then, dragging Peter out."

"Oh, come off it, Laura. He's not that malicious."

"Isn't he? I wish I could be sure. I've never told you some of the quite awful things he said to me over the months before I left. I can still hardly believe them myself. It's as though he's got something evil in him these days – and I can't imagine why, or remember when he started to change."

"But he is eighty-two – you have to make allowances..."

"No, Alan. I don't think just being old entitles anybody to be deliberately unkind, unhelpful, selfish. I don't know how your mother put up with it."

Alan shook his head.

"But he wasn't like that when she was alive. I grant you, she was always the strong one – I see that now. But he wasn't selfish, or any of the other things you accuse him of. Plain-spoken, yes, but honest – and caring. It's since Mum died that he seems to have changed, and now he just seems to be giving up..."

He stopped, tilting his head to listen. The little gong they'd left beside George's bed was clanging impatiently.

"I'll go," he said. He came down again after a few moments.

"Will you give me a hand, love, please. His bed's wet and we'll have to get him out and change everything."

Alan spent the night in a chair by his father's bed, dozing briefly between tending to the old man's needs, and thinking back to his childhood when his father had been his model, had seemed all-wise; to his rebellious adolescence when it had been imperative to escape in order to discover himself; to his twenty-third birthday on the beaches at Dunkirk, when he'd suddenly become a man. He recalled again the deep shock he'd experienced when, after Mum's death, his father had – for the first time in his life – turned to his son for advice. Now he lay here, almost totally dependent on them for his very existence. Alan rubbed his eyes. Exhaustion threatened to overtake him, but he stayed watchful.

In the morning he took Laura's breakfast to her in bed, and when she got up to put on the washing machine, he lay down fully clothed on their bed and slept immediately.

"Happy Boxing Day," muttered Laura acidly to herself as she contemplated the pile of soiled linen outside George's room. She opened his door. Lying supine, without his teeth in, his head far back on the pillows, he looked already beyond this life. She turned to go out again when she heard his whisper. She moved back towards the bed.

"Not asleep." He swallowed, and the throat-muscles strained against the flaking skin of his neck.

"Will you have a drink?"

The bony head moved fractionally from side to side.

"You should at least be trying to drink, even if you won't eat." Laura spoke gently, his vulnerability reaching her.

"No point. Go sooner if I 'ave nowt. And you'll be better pleased."

She bit back the response which flared in her mind, and held on to pity. Picking up the glass of fruit juice she lifted his head and put it to his lips. He took a little, and let the rest run down his chin. She wiped it dry.

"Try and get some sleep. I'll bring you up some soup for lunch."

Still he hadn't opened his eyes. She plumped up his pillows and left the room, gathering up the washing as she went.

At Moortop the festivities had jollied their way self-consciously through the usual rituals. A few members of a chapel choir had sung carols on each landing. Father

Christmas, his red robes and white beard just failing to conceal the identity of Irene Gifford's young nephew, had nervously dispensed toiletries, cigarettes and sweetmeats from the head of an entourage of senior staff and local dignitaries.

Dietary rules had been temporarily relaxed resulting in the night staff having their busiest night of the year. The day staff had compensated for having to be on duty while their families were celebrating by substituting a variety of refreshment for their break-time cups of tea. Some of the non-nursing staff had found innumerable reasons for needing to visit those areas where there were the amplest supplies of alcohol.

Margaret, due for her share of time off duty from midday on Boxing Day, had been relieved to observe that Irene, possibly constrained by the presence of her nephew and of a larger than usual influx of visitors, official and otherwise, appeared to be in one of her "clear" phases.

Aunt Jane was staying with Eva for a week, and Margaret set out that afternoon for Sheffield where they were postponing their Christmas until she should join them. Her mother's serenity together with Aunt Jane's bubbling anecdotes would be a fitting combination for a relaxing break.

Chapter 9

"I'm still relieved that Dad's here, rather than in Moortop," said Alan as they walked down the steps from Barford General Hospital, where George had been admitted early in the New Year. "I know it's just lingering prejudice on my part, and I'm not proud of it, but I'd have hated it if he'd gone Up the Hill."

Laura took his hand.

"I know. Obviously I'm less bothered than you are, but don't forget, if they get him over this infection he might well be sent to Moortop, at least for a time."

She felt his hand tense. In the past few days, with the house to themselves, their restored ease with each other had enabled some recovery of the old unity. But despite having talked long into the nights following George's departure, attempting to find the reasons for the near destruction of their marriage they still had not found many answers.

They had, however, established a mutual confidence which they believed would survive his return, should he recover. Alan particularly, in his meticulous way, had tried to leave no aspect unconsidered of the three-way relationship between them. Laura felt, perhaps simply because they had talked so exhaustively, or perhaps because pressures had been temporarily lifted, that although she did not welcome the possible return of the jaggedness which seemed to permeate life when her father-in-law was about, she now had the reserves to cope with it

"There's Margaret Bennett," she said as they drove onto the Delton Road out of Barford. Alan pulled up and the figure at the bus-stop ran towards them.

"Can we give you a lift?" Laura opened the rear door.

"Thanks. Mine's in for service," said Margaret as she got in. "Lucky for me you came by."

"We've been visiting Alan's father – I expect you've heard he's quite ill."

"Yes, Edna told me you'd had a rather rough Christmas. I'm sorry."

There was a short silence as Alan stopped at a pedestrian crossing, and then he said suddenly:

"I know it isn't the done thing to talk shop when you're off duty – I know I cuss to myself when parents tackle me about their kids' problems anywhere off school premises. But yes, it has been pretty grim for some time with Dad – not only since this illness, and I'd like to ask you..."

Laura interrupted him.

"Alan, love, it really isn't fair to bring this up with Margaret..."

"No Laura, I really don't mind," said Margaret. "It often helps to talk, and as Mr Hancock isn't a Moortop patient it's not a question of being unprofessional."

"He might be one soon, if they transfer him," said Laura.

"Well he isn't yet, as Miss Bennett says. And in any case I'm only talking in general terms. You've got a lot of experience with old people of all kinds – and probably with many of their families as well, and I'd very much like to hear what you think is the reason some of us have difficulties when we have to cope with them. We really did try to do our best, but it didn't work. I suppose you know about it nearly finishing our marriage, having him with us. It probably would have done, too, except for this illness. That sounds dramatic, but it's true."

Laura, listening, was astonished to realise that even yet she hadn't appreciated the full extent of Alan's hurt. Six months ago he would never have opened up like this, even to close friends, let alone to a complete stranger.

"My personal feeling," Margaret was saying, "is that with the sort of problem I think you're talking about, guilt can be very unproductive. In any situation if our best efforts don't work, feeling guilty doesn't help to find another way of tackling the problem. I know it's a cliché but it's nevertheless true, that old people often hit out hardest at those who are closest to them. The idea that all old ladies are sweet and kind and gentle and all old men are grateful or amusing or stoical, is one that should have been strangled at birth."

"I've no illusions on that score," said Laura. "The thing that's surprised me most – and I don't like to admit it – is that I've become almost hard, at the very least indifferent – about someone who's old and ill and clearly not happy."

"Surely everyone has a strong instinct for self-preservation, but we all react in our own way – and not always commendably – when it's threatened."

Margaret felt she might be treading on dangerous ground now, and Alan's next words confirmed it.

"I think we'd better leave it there," he said. "Laura was quite right – I shouldn't have raised such a personal subject. Thanks for your comments, anyway. Where can we drop you – shall I run you up to Moortop?"

Laura was someone she could get on with, Margaret decided as she said goodbye to them; about Alan she was less sure. But without doubt George Hancock had, probably unwittingly, been the catalyst for a situation in which all three of them were equally victims.

As February began, Hugh and Linda were dipping their toes into the waters which had all but engulfed Alan and Laura. So far, Flo's arrival into their home had seemed to need less adjustment than they had anticipated. Linda, at first nervous of the responsibility they had assumed, quickly became aware of her mother-in-law's determination to be as independent as her condition allowed.

"She even managed to do some of her own bits of washing today while I was out," she told Hugh one evening. "Goodness knows how she did it with that hand and arm of hers still so weak."

Hugh basked in reflected credit.

"We Spendloves never did like to be beholden," he said. "Mark my words, she'll be back in Station Street before you can say 'knife'."

"She's very quiet though, isn't she? Hasn't got much to say for herself when we're all together."

"After-effects of the stroke – bound to make a difference, especially as she still has one or two problems with her speech. Once she gets a bit stronger there'll be no stopping her."

Flo could hear the sound of their voices, though not the words, as she got herself ready for bed in the next room. This had been turned into a bed-sitting-room, a little domain which she could for the time being call her own, and she spent a good deal of each day in here. Undressing was agonisingly slow, but at least she no longer had to ask Laura to help her. She struggled to take off her stockings without overbalancing off the edge of the bed, and at the same time she talked in a semi-whisper, trying to make her lips and tongue form the words clearly, the way they'd taught her Up the Hill.

Having lived through two world wars, losing a father in one and a brother and husband in the other, she had long since ceased to believe in a benevolent deity; nevertheless she was, she supposed, offering some kind of prayer.

"Please God let me go on getting stronger with each day. May I soon be well enough to get back on my own. I suppose they're doing their best as they see it, and I know it's wrong of me not to be more grateful to them for having me here, but please don't let it be for much longer."

The door opened and Linda and Hugh put their

heads round.

"Sure you're all right, Mother? We're off upstairs now. Ring your bell if you want us in the night."

The same words, every night. And yet the empty ritual was almost comforting in its sameness. It left her free to go on following her own thoughts as she answered. She switched off the side light and lay wondering how Maureen was, and remembering the short life she'd had with Bill before he was killed, and wishing her sister Ethel hadn't died so young. Daylight seemed a long way off.

"Ey-up then, Joe. Come on nah, sit thee dahn an' dunna tek all day abaht it. I'm waiting on me breakfast, even if yo' dunna want any."

Eddie had raised his voice to make himself heard above the rattle of cutlery, the clatter of plates, the grunting and coughing, the scraping of heavy footwear on the floorboards of the dining-room. The residents of The House were preparing to stoke themselves up for another day of boredom, inertia and time-passing.

Joe Bird belied his name. He was a gaunt-faced man, his lanky limbs in the ill-fitting suit showing nothing now of the muscular strength they had once held. He pulled out the last empty chair and sat down to join his table companions. The food trolley, pushed slowly along by an elderly attendant, rumbled towards their table as Eddie noisily banged a spoon on the formica surface, shouting:

"Get a move on – that'll be cowd by t'time we get at it..."

He stopped as Miss Frost walked towards their table.

"Good morning everyone. Everything all right here?"

Only Joe spoke: "Mornin' M'h Froht. Yeh Hank hew."

Anyone unfamiliar with Joe would have been hard pressed to make any sense of his impeded speech.

Harriet Frost nodded and moved on to the next table, where she paused to reprimand Ada, who was swearing at Martha for taking too much sugar. Both the swearing and the reproach were automatic and the interchange had the weary tone of long accustomed repetition. Even so Joe, his back to them both, hinted his disturbance as he moved restlessly on the hard metal chair.

"Nah then, Joe, sit still or ye'll 'ave yer tea ovver."

To Joe, Eddy's bullying was as familiar as Ada's colourful language; but his breakfast was now spoiled, and he was first out of the dining room, shambling his way back to the dayroom to await the day's lack of eventfulness.

Sitting stiffly in an armchair he looked out at the late winter morning through the panes of a glass-panelled door, which led onto the grounds at the side of the building. He watched sparrows and starlings fighting for a share of the scraps which the attendants were throwing out from the breakfast plates. Then he looked across the low wall and the river valley to where the land rose again to merge into the Pennines. A harrowing machine was making tracks in preparation for the spring sowings.

Gradually the dayroom filled up. Men were settling themselves with a paper, a cigarette, a pipe or two, or just their thoughts. Each in his own chair, and although they exchanged the odd word, they sat isolated as though they might have been in separate rooms.

On his weekly visits Martin usually chatted briefly to several of his old friends, and then sat down to talk at greater length with one of them. Today he came over to Joe. It had taken patience and not a little effort on Martin's part to encourage him to talk. Even now it wasn't easy to catch all he said, but he could generally understand enough to conduct a conversation which they both enjoyed.

Now, Joe nodded in response to Martin's greeting and gestured towards the tractor turning on the hill.

"Did you ever drive one, Joe?"

The old man shook his head, and painfully striving to get the words out plainly, told Martin how the farm he'd worked had been flat – easier ploughing and sowing than it must be up on that hillside, even with the newfangled machines. Horses, it'd been in his day – great strong Shires, tossing and pulling. Close to them, he'd been, closer than to any humans he'd ever known, save Mam and Dad, and of course...

He stopped. Couldn't say anything to this young chap, friendly as he was, about Ellen. Martin waited, and when Joe said no more he volunteered:

"It must have been a hard life – I don't think I'd be much good at it."

Some folks think so, Joe struggled on. But he'd been happy enough as a lad. Always felt part of things then, knowing the ways of the weather and the little wild creatures all around. He told Martin how at reaping time they'd leave a few stalks standing for the harvest mice and their nests; how everyone watched for the first swallows bringing in summer; how he'd listened to the corncrakes calling along the river. He stopped speaking again, remembering that he'd never once heard them after the year Mum died.

Thinking that perhaps so much talking – more than Martin had ever heard Joe manage before – had strained the old man, he stood up and shook his hand.

Alone once more Joe shut his eyes, watching the picture-show inside his own head which was more real to him than anything that happened here. There was Ellen, laughing and flinging back her head. If she'd been there still when Mam and Dad died, he'd never have ended up in this place, stuck in all day with the rotten smells of stale tobacco smoke and yesterday's meals, and his own fusty body smell. They'd have been out in the fields, breathing sweet air. She'd have helped him keep the cottage going, even if he'd had to leave the farm job when he got too old.

Hadn't she ever understood how much he'd needed her, right from the start? She'd been close enough at first, in the early days. Fact was, *she'd* led *him* on, not t'other way round. He saw her red hair, sturdy figure, and even now, nigh on fifty years after, the image and the memory of her soft full flesh stirred him so that he found it hard to breathe. The way she'd teased and coaxed him into thinking he was all she'd ever wanted in a man!

And he'd loved her, cheat, harlot though she was. Might have known she wouldn't reckon much to the notion of staying close for good, the way he'd wanted it, not to a chap who couldn't talk right. She'd upped and left the village to marry a shop assistant in town, and he'd been left with the horses and Mam and Dad for the only real feelings he was ever to know. He could see his Mam and Dad clearly – saying little, only their pale blue eyes telling him they understood.

He'd watched them both die, within a few months of each other, worn out by their labours. On his own, try as might be, in the end he'd not been able to manage and as the cottage went more and more to the dogs, and ruin came in through the bedroom ceilings, he'd taken to living downstairs. Began to get that nothing seemed to matter any more – no point in trying to keep either the place or himself up to scratch. Then he got ill, and cold and hungry, and old Tom the milkman had shouted at him through the window.

Next thing he knew he was in hospital, and now here he was, stuck for the rest of his days in the Union, where his Mam and Dad had always feared having to end up. Praise be, that'd never happened to them, any road.

There was a clattering at the door. Joe's picture-show stopped. Miss Frost was pushing in the drugs trolley.

Harriet began the round of pain-killers, water-pills and all the other agents by which those worn and weary bodies were enabled to maintain some kind of functioning. Throughout their waking hours, only the occasional flash of temper or a lewd exchange would indicate the frustrated life-force still flickering beneath the apathy.

That flicker in Joe's particular frame suddenly became an agitation so vigorous that he almost cried out.

Ellen! There she was, behind Miss Frost. No wrinkles on her round face, no grey in her fiery hair, limbs still strong, as if...

"This is Heather, everyone." Miss Frost had raised her voice. "She's a student and she'll be helping us for a few weeks until summer. I want you all to behave well when she's about – you'll have to try extra hard not to use any dirty language or habits in front of her."

Heather? Ellen? Joe couldn't look up as Miss Frost, smarmy smile on hard face, brought the girl to each of them to tell her their names. They'd gone past now. He risked a quick glance sideways, heard "Hello, Joe". Couldn't be...

For the rest of the day Joe was even quieter than usual, although he had learned through the years of stumbling speech that you could get by with a minimum of words.

In the afternoon, as he sat in the same chair watching the daylight fade, he saw the red-haired girl climbing the hill on the other side of the river, past the farm buildings, up towards the top road. His brain, its reactions slowed down and sluggish from years of disuse, began to labour; by bedtime his plan was born.

He lay on his bed in the long dormitory. The last routines of the day were being completed. John, the night attendant, walked slowly between the beds exchanging a few words with those men still awake, and giving the last tablets to those on his treatment list. Joe lay shamming sleep.

That was the light switch going off, the door catch slotting in. Not long to wait now, but better not to move till John had finished his rounds. Snores and coughs all round him – good cover for when he had to open the door. No need to rush – he'd got all night. Listen hard. Another few minutes – John's footsteps going past again, down from the top floor; he'd be settling down now for an hour or two's break. The springs of the bed creaked as he moved – wait – nobody's woken up. Socks out of the locker, jacket off the hook behind it. Getting used to the darkness, carefully, slowly, towards the door.

Outside on the stone landing, easier to see here. Light from an open door on the floor below just reaching the top of the stairway. Hold on to the iron handrail – now, slowly down the stairs.

Dance music playing on John's wireless – good. Still, passing that open door would be the trickiest bit. Wait here, in the corner. John whistling the tune with the wireless. A newspaper rustling. Better risk it before the midnight pill round was due. Not moved so fast for years – across the beam of light and he was on his way down the next flight to the ground floor. That outside door now, it squeaked; and what about the sound of the key turning? The bolt sliding? He waited again, sweating a little, but cold. Suddenly from the second floor landing, the one right at the top, Charlie was hollering – praise be, the poor old feller was having one of his fits. As if he wanted to help...

Joe opened the door, stepped out and closed it again quietly. He stood for a moment in the chill night air. The first deep breath made him feel a little giddy and he leaned against the coldness of the stone wall. He looked up at the black sky and then edged along the first yard. Keeping in the deepest shadow until he was clear of The House he hurried down the path by the lawns. He went round to the far side of the old hut before climbing stiffly over the low wall and dropping down into long wet grass on the other side.

His socks were quickly soaked, but he noticed neither this nor the sharpness of the night breeze through his thin pyjama trousers. Returning along the line of the wall he stumbled down the steep, hedge-lined track, brambles catching at his jacket, until at last he reached the wooden footbridge over the river. The wind was rising now and blowing bleakly down the water course.

In the middle of the first field under the hillside, Joe stopped once, looking up the slope into the darkness.

"Ellen!" he shouted, and then again, "Ellen!"

A horse at the far end of the field, startled, stamped its hooves and whinnied. Joe walked on.

As the news fluttered through The House after breakfast the next morning there were few comments. Joe, more than most, had always walked alone. They had found his body astride a stone wall at the top of the hill on the far side of the river, his hands cradled tightly round either end of a smooth through-boulder.

Whilst the formalities were being dealt with by Mr Barraclough, Miss Gifford and Harriet Frost, Margaret walked quietly through the dayrooms. She felt a tug at her elbow. Martha, hairy chin thrust forward, tiny eyes glinting, moved closer. Her podgy fingers indicated first her crotch and then the side of her forehead.

"Allus said 'e'd more down there than up 'ere," she growled.

Margaret looked at her, and experienced a momentary feeling of kinship with this almost repellently unattractive old woman. And at the same time she thought she could even understand why poor Joe had gone searching for a wraith in the cold midnight. Does it never die, she wondered, this gaping need in those of us who have never passed anything of ourselves on through children?

When Martin left his books to answer the phone that afternoon, he was surprised to hear Grace's voice.

"I wanted to tell you before you saw it in the Gazette," she said. "I saw you chatting with Joe yesterday when I passed the dayroom window." She went on to explain as much as was known of what had happened, ending: "You must have been one of the last people he spoke to, really talked, I mean. It'll be a hospital funeral – I'll let you know when, if you're interested."

"Thanks. Yes, please. I'd like to go. It's good of you to think of ringing."

He replaced the receiver wondering at the intensity of his sense of loss.

Chapter 10

Harriet was late getting home. Joe Bird's death the previous night and the consequent disruption of routine during the day had caused her to miss her usual bus, and it was past six o'clock when she reached the house. Her mother made no comment on the time, but brought two bowls through from the kitchen as Harriet sat down at the table.

"Not stew again, Mother, for pity's sake! That's the second time in a week. Even Moortop can do better than that."

She regarded the dish in front of her with an expression of mild outrage, as though its contents offered a personal insult.

Carrie Frost's hand, the soup-spoon already lifted halfway to her mouth, began to tremble so that brown droplets spilled onto the white table-cloth.

"Now look what you've done!"

Harriet got up and went into the kitchen, returning with a damp cloth with which she tried to wipe up the spots.

"There's no help for it. I suppose I'll have to set to each week and make out menus and shopping lists for you, and then perhaps we'll get some decent meals."

Her mother had stopped eating and was watching Harriet's every move.

"Well, get on with it." Harriet sat down again. "We may as well eat it now you've made it. No sense in wasting it. I can't stand waste."

Carrie continued to stare at her daughter as they resumed the meal, her hand steadier but a muscle in her lined cheek twitching irregularly.

They had cleared away and were sitting in the two fireside chairs with their cups of tea before Carrie spoke for the first time since dishing up meal. Her voice was high and soft.

"Has it been a hard day, Hatty?"

"Of *course* it's been a hard day. It always is a hard day, trying to keep up some kind of decent standards with that lot – if they're not stupid they're crafty; the men are mostly disgusting and a good many of the women aren't much better. And then one silly old fool has to get out in the night and die from exposure."

Carrie began to say something, but Harriet disregarded her.

"They're all so ungrateful, that's what gets me. Everything done for them and yet they're always grumbling. And how many times do I have to ask you not to call me Hatty. You named me Harriet, and I wish you'd stick to it."

Her mother, arthritis joints cracking, levered herself slowly out of her chair and went to wash up.

"Make sure the water's good and hot – that stew was very greasy," Harriet called after her as she picked up her library book.

It was nearly an hour before Carrie came back into the living room. She sat for a time staring into the fire, and occasionally looking round at the meticulous neatness of the little room. Once, she bent awkwardly forward to pick a strand of cotton from the hearth-rug.

When Harriet switched on the radio for the main evening news, her mother got up and said quietly:

"I'll go up now, then, Harriet. Goodnight, dear. I hope you sleep well."

"Goodnight. Don't forget, to take your tablets."

Harriet heard the headlines and the first news item, and then she turned the radio off again and sat, listening to each sound of her mother's preparations for bed. The thin walls of the pre-war council house allowed its occupants no real privacy, even for the most intimate of activities.

When she heard the light switch click off in the room above, she picked up the evening paper.

The front page blazed at her:

"Man accused of raping young girl."

Her limbs stiffened and her stomach contracted. She threw down the paper and rushed into the kitchen where she vomited violently into the sink.

When her trembling subsided and the cold dampness no longer crept across her forehead she went back into the living-room and sat down, but she did not relax. It was anger now that tensed her long-boned, angular body.

A six-word headline had been sufficient to spring yet again the lid of the cess-pit which she had striven for nearly forty years to keep tightly shut. Mostly these days her rigid control was successful, but she would never be certain what incident, remark, sight or sound might release the stream of noxious filth to gush up and disrupt the ordered regularity of her life.

This time, though, the words of that headline were so brutal a reminder that she was powerless against the images which forced themselves at her. First, the darkened bedroom where she had lain, a lonely, puzzled child, on the night of her eleventh birthday, her mother away in hospital for what Harriet had been told was "a big operation", the overheard whispered references to "having it all taken away" serving only to increase her apprehension about what was being done to her mother, and leading her to wonder fearfully in what way she would be different when she came back.

Then followed the crack of light from the landing as the bedroom door had opened, and next, her father's heavy figure, a black silhouette on the threshold. His voice had been somehow different from usual – thick, yet quiet, as he'd asked her why she was still awake.

Even now, at forty-seven, she still tended to tremble

and retch as the next image overwhelmed her: her father suddenly bending over her bed, muttering about another birthday present, a special one, just from him – no need to tell Mummy about it when she came home. There had been pain, a suffocating weight, more pain, and yet more; and then he had slumped down on the floor beside the bed while she had lain torn and bruised, sticky and bleeding, and cold to the core of her terrified self.

Afterwards there had been days, weeks, when she had prayed over and over that he would go away, be drowned, murdered, run over, so that she need never again see his coarse-veined red face, or the shifty blue eyes that hadn't once looked directly at her after that night. She had welcomed her mother's return from hospital because she felt that in some obscure way he'd not ever again be sure whether Harriet would keep his secret.

At last, now, she reached the only memory she could willingly embrace – the triumph of her prayers answered on that afternoon, years later, when she'd arrived home from her last day at school to find her mother weeping, telling her between maudlin sobs that he'd left them and wouldn't be coming back. She had felt no compassion, no pity, only a hard joy for herself and contempt for her mother for having allowed herself to be contaminated by such a creature.

The clock over the fireplace struck eleven and Harriet, calm again, stood up. She straightened the cushions on both chairs; took the evening paper, by now screwed into a tight ball, out to the dustbin; gave the kitchen sink a further swilling with disinfectant, and checked that her mother had prepared her sandwiches for the following day.

As she undressed, carefully folding each garment, she wondered why she stayed at Moortop. If Margaret Bennett were eventually to take charge she'd make life a lot more difficult than the Gifford did these days. She could always go back to private work – her war-time qualifications were still acceptable for that. She'd have less responsibility, only herself to answer for. There were going to be changes soon anyway, with re-organisation. On the other hand she could at least delegate quite a lot in her present position, the pay wasn't too bad, and there was security. Besides, with private patients you couldn't always be sure how far you'd be able actually to take charge of things, whereas for the moment at Moortop you could keep some sort of hold on the reins. Better the devil you knew... She smoothed her pillow and prepared for sleep.

Carrie, although she had not forgotten her sleeping tablet, nor the arthritis pills, was still awake when Harriet came to bed. She lay with eyes closed, just in case her daughter should look in. Not that she ever had yet, not in thirty years, but with Harriet you never knew. For the thousandth time (more than that: how many days *were* there in more than thirty years?) she asked herself how it could happen that a mother and daughter could live together and yet be total strangers, and so unhappy.

How could the affectionate, carefree little girl Hatty had once been have turned into such a cold, bitter and eternally criticising woman? Time and again Carrie had wondered where she'd failed her only child. Once upon a time she used to blame Albert's desertion, imagining it was because the girl had had no father after she was fourteen, but then she'd realised, looking back, that Harriet had changed long before he went. She'd gone quiet and sulky, scarcely exchanging a word with either of them. And why hadn't she had friends, like any normal child? Never asked anyone home, never hinted at a boyfriend, nor asked a thing about her father when he left. And in the days when she'd still tried to talk to her, mother to daughter, any questions about that sort of thing had led to rows, or to even longer than usual cold silences, and Carrie had finally stopped trying to get near her.

She sighed deeply, and turned over carefully so as not to let Harriet hear that she was still awake. She wondered how long you could keep going without proper, regular sleep. For years now she'd not been able to decide which she dreaded most – going to bed each night to lie awake thinking how much Harriet seemed to resent her, hate her, even perhaps wish her dead; or getting up each morning, still tired, to a day to be spent making sure that there would be nothing, no tiny mistake or omission in her running of the house (she certainly didn't think of it as a home) that could annoy Harriet, set her off on a catalogue of fault-finding, like the disaster of the stew this evening.

What was the point of such a life? She had precious few friends left, and rarely saw any of them. She went nowhere except down to the shops and back, and to Chapel on Sunday night if the pain wasn't too bad.

She wondered if Harriet was asleep yet; whether she dared turn on her bedside lamp and read her magazine. The luminous hands of the alarm clock told her it was after midnight. She'd risk it. She muffled the light switch with her handkerchief. The concentrated circle of brightness cast by the small lamp dazzled her temporarily, and she squinted at the base of its stem until her vision steadied. Bright splashes of light were reflected back from the glass of the two bottles of tablets.

"It is dangerous to exceed the stated dose."

There's always that, thought Carrie. And if it should mean eternal damnation, well, there's more than one sort of hell. Not tonight, though. Even at her threescore years and ten she wasn't quite beaten yet. But one day, perhaps... She began to read the short story.

Chapter 11

Martin had agreed, though with some reservation, to Margaret's suggestion that he might like to join the residents' Whit-week outing to the seaside.

"The staff'll be glad of an extra pair of hands," she told him. "You can never have too much help on these trips, and with your knowing so many of the men the attendants will be pleased to have you with them."

He wasn't so sure. He thought they might well resent an outsider tagging along, but it might be one of his last opportunities for close contact with his old friends in The House, and it would be a welcome break from his concentrated revision for the approaching exams.

The coach was standing in the front yard when he turned in at the gate, and one or two of the women were already in their seats, dressed in their best clothes, their faces shiny with soap and excitement. He spoke to Grace, who had come in early to help to get the less mobile ones aboard, and then he went to look for Miss Frost and Ken Batty, who were in charge of the arrangements.

It took over half an hour to get everybody settled, by which time the ones who had been in their places first had to get out again for another visit to the lavatory.

Eventually they were on their way, the arguments about who should sit where, the protests about sticks and coats being put up onto the luggage rack, gradually subsiding into occasional spurts of talk and laughter.

The men were all at the rear of the vehicle, the women in the front – an arrangement which to Martin seemed faintly ridiculous. He was sitting with Robert, trying to encourage him to talk about his singing days, but Robert was being more than usually taciturn. Martin turned to listen to Eddie, on the other side of the gangway, reminiscing about Sunday School outings of his boyhood.

"Ponies and traps we went in, scores of us, up to t'Dales. I alwuz won in t'three-legged races, only they'd never let me 'ave me leg tied to a lass's. That'd've been summat like, eh?" His wheezy chuckle was infectious, and Martin laughed. "Ginger beer and meat-paste sandwiches, we 'ad. Never tasted ginger beer like it since. Grand, it were." He smacked his lips at the memory.

There was a sort of grunt at Martin's shoulder, and he looked up into the round pink face of Billy Pearson. Dumbo ears stuck out beneath a monk-like tonsure of yellow hair, but the deep-set eyes looked anything but holy.

"Where are you off to, Willy?" asked Martin, his hand on the man's sleeve.

"Want to sit wi' Poll." Willy shook Martin's hand off impatiently, and pushed forward, stumbling as the coach rounded a bend.

"Now come on, Willy, go and sit down in your own seat. There's no room at the front." Martin stood up and began to follow Willy. By this time Ken Batty was blocking the gangway in front of them, and Harriet was standing behind Ken.

"Get back to your seat at once, William Pearson." Her raised voice splashed like a cold shower over the cosy little world of the coach. Ken turned Willy round, urging him back to his place as Martin sat down again. Polly Mason's faded prettiness flushed scarlet as she kept her head turned towards the window. At her side Phoebe whimpered quietly and trembled a little.

No-one spoke for a short time, and then Eddie suddenly called out, turning his head, "Good try, Willy lad, good try!" One or two of the men laughed uncertainly, and a kind of damp normality returned to the company.

It was striking twelve when the coach passed the resort's Victorian Clock Tower and as they travelled slowly along the promenade some of those on the side away from the beach tried to stand up to catch a glimpse of the sea. The attendants worried at them to stay seated for fear of falling, and by the time they reached the coach-park nearly everyone was in a state of agitation.

Getting the party to the fish-and-chip restaurant for the pre-ordered lunch was easier than Martin had envisaged. Having breakfasted early, they were all now hungry and at the mention of food they flocked eagerly along in the wake of Ken Batty and Elsie Blake, while Harriet chivvied the few stragglers at the rear.

The pink-mirrored walls of the restaurant caused some embarrassment to those sitting near them. Unused to watching themselves or their companions eating, some sat open-mouthed in fascination; others averted their faces and attempted to speed up the process to get it over. Eddie was among the first to clear his plate. He sat back and belched contentedly.

"Wot's for afters, then?" he enquired of no-one in particular.

A large, middle-aged waitress, frizzy brown nest of hair piled above her tired, pudgy face, shuffled on veined legs between the tables. Eddie watched her, and as she passed he leaned out to pat her buttocks. If she felt the contact she chose not to react and Martin, sitting at the adjoining table, was relieved that he didn't need to intervene. Eddie caught his look, and winked.

After the meal, and much checking and re-checking that nobody was left behind in the toilets, the party was shepherded across the promenade on to the beach. Most of them, tired now, settled awkwardly into deck-chairs to doze, or to stare at the waves and at the few early holiday-makers. Mad Phoebe set off to look for her cats; Robert gazed at the distant pier, perhaps trying to recall whether The Thirties Follies had ever had a booking there; Anne Prince watched the donkeys; one or two of the more active women were down at the water's edge, shoes and stockings off, dipping their feet into the shallows. Although the sun shone, a chill sea-breeze blew across the sands, and the women shivered in their summer clothes.

Harriet Frost and Ken Batty went off with two more staff to buy ice-creams for everyone and Martin, becoming aware of the thinning of the supervision, repeatedly ticked off in his mind those he could be sure had been on the coach. He thought of Joe, and wished he could have been with them.

He began to walk slowly among the deck-chairs as the minutes passed, and Harriet and the others still had not returned. Looking over towards the promenade at the point where they had left the beach, he saw Polly Mason ambling across the sand, her face red and her hair slightly dishevelled. Her blouse and cardigan, too, were unusually untidy for her. Elsie Blake was joining her.

"Where've you been, Polly? Are you all right?" she was asking as Martin turned back to the others.

"Just for a bit of a walk," he heard her say.

The ice-creams arrived and were handed out. There were two surplus.

"Who's not had one?" called Ken.

"I haven't." Willy Pearson appeared as if from nowhere, and Martin realised that he had not been there when he'd last done a mental check. He handed Willy the cornet that Harriet passed to him, the contents by now nearly melted.

Harriet and Ken made another round of their charges, with the last ice-cream collapsing soggily into mush in Ken's hand.

"Gladys" exploded Harriet. "Gladys Chapman – where is she?" Everyone began to look around them, and then Harriet's face took on a red, "I knew it" look. She turned to Ken Batty.

"I said all along we ought never to have let either Willy or Gladys come. There's always some sort of trouble when they're about. We'll have to go and look for her. If we're not back within half an hour, Mrs Blake, you and the others get everyone back to the coach. We'll meet you there as soon as we find Gladys – we're due to leave at four."

A shudder of excitement ran through those left on the sands. They drew closer together, standing about in little groups or sitting uncomfortably upright in the deck-chairs. Only Mad Phoebe was off again on her eternal quest, this time towards the breakwater, quietly calling "Puss, puss".

Elsie Blake took a large beach ball out of her holdall and blew it up, and then attempted to organise a simple round game with anyone who would join in. Martin went off to keep an eye on Mad Phoebe. A family party was gathering up its belongings when she passed them, and one of the children danced behind her, mimicking her "Puss, puss". As Martin neared them, he heard the mother say: "They shouldn't be allowed to bring such people into public places. What can you expect?" And a little farther on, before he reached Phoebe, he saw a group of teenagers giggling at her, and then at him as he tried to coax her back to the others. He looked in their direction and then covertly at Phoebe. They were not much younger than he and for a second he saw the whole gathering through their eyes and flushed. He hurried Mad Phoebe back towards the main party.

The search for Gladys Chapman ended in the post-office. A bewildered young clerk had spent some time trying to deal with Gladys's frenetic demands that a telegram be sent to her uncle in South Africa who was investing in gold mines on her behalf. She had produced from her handbag several "certificates" and on the clerk's discovery that these documents were, in fact, pieces of carefully folded toilet paper the police had been called. Gladys, by now in tears and very subdued, was led back to the coach-park where the remainder of the party were becoming restless. As she was pushed up the steps and into her seat by Harriet, Martha called out:

"Silly cow. We shouldn't have brought you with us."

As the coach started, others took up the taunts, and Gladys began to weep afresh.

The return journey was comparatively uneventful. A stop for drinks and crisps was followed, as they set off again, by Eddie's attempting to get a sing-song going among the men. Robert stayed silent but the rest joined in "I do like to be beside the seaside" whilst the women wavered their way through "Only a bird in a gilded cage".

It was nearly dark when the coach turned into Moortop, and Martin felt as though he had done a week's hard labour. He stood by the steps helping the passengers down. One of the last to get off was Willy, and as he walked away something fell from inside his jacket. Martin picked it up and was about to call after Willy when he realised, in a rush of embarrassment, that it was a women's undergarment of some kind.

"Thank you for your help, Martin." Harriet was standing behind him. "You've seen for yourself now, I hope, that looking after people like this is anything but a picnic."

"I never thought it was," he replied. "But I'm glad I came. Do you need any more help? If not, I'll be getting along. Oh, by the way, I found this." He pushed the garment into her hands and hurried away before she could respond.

Polly Mason was admitted to Robin Ward the following day with a chest cold and a slight fever, but was back in The House by the end of a week. Willy Pearson was observed to be rather more restless and troublesome than usual for several days. The matter of the stray camisole was never satisfactorily explained.

Chapter 12

The Gifford Scandal broke only a few days before the annual Garden Party at the end of May. Late one evening a small fire broke out in the kitchen between the two small flats in which Irene and Margaret lived. A towel had been put to dry near the boiler, and had begun to smoulder. The porter on his round of the grounds smelled the smoke and raised the alarm. When the Fire Brigade, as a precaution, set in motion the temporary evacuation of the premises it proved impossible to rouse Irene Gifford.

Margaret confirmed that she had seen her return to her flat earlier that evening from a day off, and had since heard her moving about. Eventually, with the police in attendance, the locked door was forced and firemen had found her, empty gin bottle at her side, so heavily asleep that they were unable to wake her.

There was no way the affair could be totally suppressed, although efforts were made to cloak the truth with official reports of sudden illness, more serious than her previous "indispositions". Margaret was deputed to take charge of Moortop pending the enquiry and Irene, suspended from duty, went to stay with friends.

The gossip so endemic to institutions was, to Margaret's relief, overtaken by preparations for what was regarded by most people in any way connected with Moortop, as The Event of the year.

A haze over the river just after dawn promised fine weather, and by breakfast time the sun was already warming the stone-faced walls on the south side of the buildings. Benches and trestle tables lined the edges of the main lawn; bunting, strung between trees and the tops of convenient fire-escapes, fluttered slightly in the faintest of breezes.

By mid-morning, watched by some of the more

mobile inhabitants of The House (who often enjoyed this part of the proceedings more than the afternoon itself), stall-holders were already at work decorating their tables and carrying cartons and baskets and trays of merchandise to stow away under covers. A group of boys from the Delton Lads' Brigade were carrying chairs and setting them round the display area, where later the local dancing school and the Barford Town Band would perform.

The most detailed and complicated preparation, however, was being devoted to The Platform, which had been erected from large trestles, to be reached by means of a small portable staircase brought from the hall.

This construction was now being covered with a carpet, taken out of store once a year for the occasion. Shouts and curses were exchanged by the porters as they struggled to get the covering straight, with sufficient material hanging down at the front to disguise the supports, but not so much that the whole thing might slip off the planks. Troughs of plants stood about them as they worked, and when one of them was kicked over the vehemence of their oaths caused the ladies working on the cake stall nearby to tut in confusion. Eddie, playing his own private game of being the gaffer, added his gleeful shouts to those of the workers.

At last it was ready, chairs for the officials in place, banks of flowers on every available surface, table for the Opener with water-carafe at the ready.

Among the spectators of the bustling activity, one above all of them was drawn irresistibly to this important area. Anne Prince – nicknamed by staff and residents alike "The Princess of Moortop" – felt that here at last was something with which she could identify.

Anne had arrived at Moortop only in February and so had not previously experienced this annual jamboree. She was slight, delicately featured, with a transparently fair skin and light blue eyes; her whole demeanour suggesting that she felt out of place in this environment.

The others in The House had quickly become impatient with her incessant complaints. She would observe: "Of course I am accustomed to a quite different style of life"; or, "I am unused to such coarse food"; or again, "It is impossible for me to sleep properly on a hard bed in a shared room"; in fact, the others decided, she considered herself more than a little above the place and its occupants.

"My poor dear Thomas would break his heart if he could see me now," she would say, and Martha and Dolly would snigger as much at what they called her cut-glass voice, as at what it said. Most of all, Anne was resentful that even Miss Frost, and Mrs Blake, and the Matron – who were in positions of authority and should have known better – didn't seem to recognise the sort of background she came from, and treated her as though she were a born pauper. That other woman who seemed to be in some sort of charge – Bennett, she thought the name was – did address her civilly, but then so she did everyone, which surely meant she must be two-faced.

Anne knew that one thing which annoyed the staff was her wardrobe. She had managed to bring with her a comprehensive selection of clothing, and the dormitory lockers were far too small to accommodate more than a fraction of it. The majority had to be stored in a locked cupboard at the top of The House, where she had to ask to be taken so that she could make the changes of outfit which she felt were appropriate to different seasons and times of day. This morning she had selected a floral crêpe-de-chine gown which now lay draped across her bed. Regarding it earlier, she had rejoiced in the splash of colour it introduced into the drabness of the room.

When Anne's husband had committed suicide following the collapse of his business into bankruptcy, she had been devastated to learn that she was virtually destitute, even the house and furniture being taken from her to meet the demands of the many creditors' claims on Thomas's estate. The double shock had resulted in a period of treatment in a psychiatric hospital, from which she had been transferred to Moortop. Her personal clothing and jewellery were all she had left to remind her of the days of a full social diary – golf club and Rotary dinners, holidays abroad, coffee mornings and bridge evenings.

She hoarded the tiny sum allowed to her from the state pension, shocked afresh each week at how little it was, and also by this regular reminder that Thomas had not even made provision through any kind of insurance for her possible needs in such an eventuality. Although the basic necessities for survival were now guaranteed, she craved still for the luxuries to which she had been accustomed. However hard she tried to accumulate her few shillings' "pocket money" it melted away in trifles, so that things like the expensive chocolates and exclusive make-up which she loved were no longer attainable.

But today she was happy and excited. She would come into her own at the Garden Party. Her clothes would out-shine not only her companions' but those of the visitors, the staff, the lady stall-holders. And because of her carefully prepared scheme she would be able to patronise every stall as befitted one of her natural position in life. She might even get the chance to speak to the local MP who would be opening the event.

In a well-cut "everyday" summer shirt and blouse she was now making a careful tour of the grounds, noting the positions of the stalls where she would make her most important purchases and mentally selecting the most advantageous seat from which she could applaud the entertainment. She looked forward particularly to the dancing display. She had always hoped that her daughter Sarah might take up classical ballet. But Sarah had died in childhood and there had been no other children.

She returned again to the platform, admiring the potted plants banked along the front; the professional touches of the water-carafe and the microphone. She wondered whom she should approach with her request to be introduced to the opener; the former MP, Philip Harborne, had been an old friend, but his successor had been elected during the period of what she now thought of as "my troubles", and she had not met him.

The clock in the tower struck noon, and looking around her Anne realised that she was almost the only resident left outside, apart from old Mad Phoebe who was as usual peering round corners and under trees calling for her cats. She had once told Anne they were her only friends, and didn't believe they'd been put down when she'd been brought in from her caravan to Moortop.

Lunchtime had drawn all the others to the dayrooms, where they were to have an early midday snack of sandwiches and fruit, the dining hall having been appropriated for the visitors' afternoon teas. Bidding Phoebe to follow, Anne hurried indoors and made her way to join Martin and Dolly. She looked with distaste at the unappetising food on their table – sliced bread enclosing pieces of processed cheese, a bowl of floppy yellowing lettuce leaves, and a dish of hard green pears and over-ripe bananas.

Lunch over she went up to wash and change, afterwards applying rouge, powder and perfume from her rapidly dwindling supplies. Today she was extravagant and made no attempt to economise as she patted, smoothed and sprayed.

The dormitories were deserted. Not one of the other women was troubling to change; they had dressed that morning in what they would wear all day. She paused to listen as she stepped out on to the landing. Halfway down the staircase she stopped by the window and looked down into the grounds. All the staff seemed to be busy out there:

some who were off duty were arranging their own plant stall, others attending to the less mobile residents, helping them to find seats where they could sit in the sun all afternoon, knotted handkerchieves and cotton bonnets on their heads. Anne saw Miss Frost deep in conversation with a group of visitors who had arrived early.

She walked down the remaining stairs, but instead of turning towards the outer door she continued along the corridor towards the duty room. The door was closed. She knocked gently. There was no reply. She knocked again, looking up and down the corridor. Still silence. Quickly she tried the handle – the door was unlocked and she slipped inside. Less then two minutes later she emerged. The Bennett woman stood in the corridor.

"Is anything wrong, Mrs Prince? What did you want from the duty room?"

"Nothing, that is..." Anne stammered, flushed, and then said:

"A slight headache – I thought an Aspirin might help. But everyone's outside, I suppose. It's gone off now, in fact – I'm quite all right."

"Are you sure? Well, you'd better get along out there too – it's nearly time for the opening."

Anne, clutching her handbag closely under her arm, composed herself and walked out into the sunlight.

The official party was just mounting the platform as she nudged her way to the front of the crowd, choosing a spot immediately in front of the guest of honour. Miss Bennett had followed, and was now joining the officials.

The Association for Moortop Chairman – whom Anne was sure she recognised from some long past encounter – introduced the MP Ronald White in a few cool words.

How agreeable it will be, thought Anne, to hear a cultured voice again after all this time in the company of these common old men and women. She listened, unbelieving, as Mr White, his dress unconventionally informal, begun to address his audience in a broad Yorkshire accent. He spoke of his sense of privilege at being invited to support such a worthy cause.

"Our senior brothers and sisters, who've laboured so hard all their lives, are entitled to end their days in comfort, free from want or worry," he boomed, and went on to assure his listeners that all the proceeds from the day's event would help to provide these little extras which State funds had previously been unable to allow for, although he promised that his Party would keep their election pledge to increase provision for such as the men and women of Moortop. He hoped that everyone would spend until it hurt.

Anne didn't register the raised eyebrows on the faces of some of the staff and visitors as Ronald White sat down, but she was bewildered. In the natural order of things, MPs ought at least to look and sound as though they belonged to the right class. But she clapped politely; he was, after all, an MP.

The band blew the opening bars of a Sousa march and the platform party set off on the traditional buying tour before Anne could make her bid for an introduction to Ronald White. In any case she was less sure now that she wanted to meet him. She embarked on her own spending spree.

Avoiding areas where she saw members of staff, she also took care to make each purchase at times when there were several customers waiting to be served. The Bennett woman had disappeared with the other officials, and Anne felt light-hearted again as she made her way to the toiletry stall. She stood back for several minutes, delighting in the display of rich soaps, expensively packaged powder puffs and talc, and outrageously priced perfumes. When a small crush had gathered she made her selection – Elisabeth Arden face-powder, a puff, a soft pale pink face-cloth and a tiny phial of Chanel perfume. She felt a thrill of pleasure as she drew the notes from her purse, paid quickly, and dropped her purchases into the plastic carrier she had now unfolded from her handbag.

Next she went towards the sweet stall, but there were only children there at the moment so that she was conspicuous among them. She looked across the lawn at the Bargain Bran Barrel. It was worth risking a shilling or two there, just for the fun of it. Luck stayed with her and she came away after only two tries with a miniature bottle of liqueur.

At the end of half an hour her carrier was almost full, and quite heavy. She found a seat at the front of the big lawn, vacated just as the band moved away to give place to the dancing school.

The programme which followed was as pleasing as Anne had anticipated – fairies, little Dutch girls, a Snow White with her attendant dwarves, and if there were occasional wrong steps and the piano was inaudible to anyone farther from it than a few feet, that made it all the more appealing. A sentimental tear ran down her cheek. She dabbed at it with a lace-edged wisp of fine linen.

It had been a wonderful afternoon. She was even sure that Ronald White had actually smiled directly at her when the platform party had passed her near the sweet stall.

As the crowds gradually drifted away and the detritus began to blow about paths and grass and flowerbeds in a sudden breeze, the Princess of Moortop walked slowly indoors, climbed the stairs to her dormitory and pushed the plastic carrier to the back of her locker, well hidden beneath a pile of underwear.

Harriet Frost was on the bus home, her modest purchases from the day in a small string bag. Her feet ached and she was more than usually irritable. She took out her purse to pay the fare and checking the contents, tried to work out how it was that she had spent so much. She must have had many more unsuccessful goes on the tombola and the other sideshows than she had realised – there was practically nothing in her purse but small change.

Margaret, leafing through files in Matron's office late into the evening, in order to acquaint herself with some of the less familiar details of her new duties, recalled her encounter with Anne Prince. Perhaps she should make further enquiries? She was tugging at a folder which had become caught at the back of the filing cabinet. The cover tore, and freeing it she took it to the desk. The contents appeared to be mainly personal items belonging to Irene Gifford – receipts, a few greetings cards, appeal literature. She began to put them into a neat pile to be forwarded if Irene did not return.

One long envelope fell from the pile on to the floor. Margaret bent to pick it up and noticed that it was addressed to Mrs Irene Blackstone, at a hospital in Hampshire. The date on the postmark was 1953 – the year in which Irene Gifford had joined the staff at Moortop as Deputy Matron – having come, as Margaret knew, from somewhere near Winchester. Divorce? Desertion? Widowhood?

Whichever it was, the gin-bottle now made sad sense. She sat thoughtfully for a few moments, and then decided to dismiss Anne Prince's little trespass into the duty room as being too insignificant to pursue.

Chapter 13

In the bright light of high summer the flat corn-gold fields of the northern Fenlands ahead appeared to stretch to the edge of the world.

Margaret glanced at her mother, gently sleeping in the passenger seat, and stopped the green Mini at the side of the gun-metal ribbon of road, switching off the engine. This clear-lit, uncomplicated landscape of defined margins and unimpeded views attracted and soothed her. She followed the horizon round in a wide arc. In the distance, to the right, she glimpsed a round church tower above a low clump of trees. Her mother woke.

"Are we there? Sorry – I think I nodded off."

"Not for now. I'll just check." She took the map from Eva's lap and studied it for a few moments. As she handed it back to her mother, she asked:

"You're feeling all right? It's a bit farther than I thought it would be."

"Yes, I'm fine. That little nap refreshed me."

In the market-place of the small town Margaret pulled in to the kerb to ask a passer-by for directions, then drove on for another half-mile or so, eventually turning in to a smooth-surfaced drive. Trees, not yet fully mature, surrounded a large courtyard. In one corner stood an old, elegant building which must have been the original Hornlow Hall and which had now obviously been adapted for use as a staff residence. Separated from it by a wide expanse of close-cut grass was a complex of single-storey buildings extending back from either side of the double-doored entrance.

Margaret parked alongside a gleaming white, well-upholstered minibus and they got out and walked towards the bungalow buildings.

Inside, doors and passages led out of a spacious, six-sided lobby which was furnished with low tables and armchairs. In one of these sat an old man intently watching the movements of tropical fish in a large tank in an alcove; each of the wide window-sills displayed plants and flowers, and on one wall behind a highly-polished reception desk, a plaque announced that Hornlow Hall had been officially opened three years previously by a titled lady as a retirement home.

Eva looked up at Margaret and smiled, her eyes twinkling.

"Nothing but the best for Jane, as always," she whispered.

A small board on the desk requested, in gilt lettering: "Please press this button for attention". Two old ladies, one supporting herself on a walking-frame, moved slowly, past them, engrossed in their tottering progress. Margaret pressed the button and somewhere a buzzer sounded, a subdued note breaking the almost ecclesiastical hush.

Through one of the doors a young woman came towards them.

"Good afternoon. Are you visiting someone?"

As they were led along the wide corridors, Margaret noted through an open door here, a gloss panel there, the taste and the resources which had dictated the high quality of furnishing and equipment throughout this home.

Their escort stopped in front of a door on which she tapped, and then opening it she called quietly, "Mrs Reynolds, you have some visitors."

Jane, although three years younger than Eva, looked the older of the two. The time she had spent in the East had dried and yellowed her skin, and her hair was ice-white and thinning. Now Margaret also saw in her a fragility and vulnerability which had not been evident at Christmas.

On the surface her manner was as exuberant as always.

"Eva, Meg, what a lovely surprise!"

She got up, holding out both hands. The sisters embraced, and Margaret kissed the papery cheek.

"What do you think of my new home, then? Rather grand isn't it? I'll show you round later, but first we'll have a cup of tea." She opened the door of a small cupboard and lifted out what Margaret and Eva recognised as part of a fine bone china tea-service from Cliff House.

"I was told I could bring anything I liked with me, provided there was space for it. It wasn't easy to reduce from the whole of Cliff House to one room, but at least it helped me to decide once and for all what I really treasured most. And of course selling off the furniture and things provided me with an extra little nest egg. Meg, dear, would you like to make the tea? There's a little kitchen just along the corridor and you'll find my milk in the fridge in the jug from this set – we all keep our own, although sometimes I suspect some of the residents help themselves to other people's if they run short."

As Margaret took the small tray and went in search of the kitchen, Jane continued to chatter and still seemed hardly to have paused for breath when she returned.

"I was just telling your mother," she said, as Margaret set down the tray and began to pour out the tea, "the doctor here has such an unfortunate name – Graves!" Her laughter tinkled in harmony with the delicate chink of the china. "Hardly inspires confidence, does it? But he's a charming young man, perhaps a bit too young to understand how we old dodderers feel sometimes."

"I can't think of you as an old dodderer, Aunt," said Margaret.

"Well, one tries to keep up standards of course, but it's sometimes a bit of an effort. Do you know there are some of them here who don't bother to spruce themselves up, never mind actually change, for dinner?"

"Oh Jane," Eva laughed. "You don't alter, does she, Meg?"

Margaret smiled but said nothing. As the sisters chatted, she noticed that the conversation was dominated by Jane's concerns. She asked little about Eva's activities and now and again Margaret caught fleeting evidence on her aunt's face of what she had come to describe to herself as that now familiar "look of otherness". She pushed this observation away to be reconsidered later but she knew that her mother would also have realised how circumscribed Jane's world was becoming, and how little interested she already seemed in life outside of Hornlow.

Before they left, Jane took them to see some of the facilities afforded by the Home and her almost proprietorial air was a further parochial tendency uncharacteristic of the Jane of only six months before.

As they walked back to the entrance hall together they passed a number of old men and women most of whom had patently been conditioned to a lifetime of well-being such as could scarcely be imagined by most of their contemporaries in Moortop and yet to Margaret many of them bore in their faces the same stigmata of that visitation upon the old which so teased her interest.

Once they had left the flat lands behind them and were travelling the more familiar roads taking them back to Sheffield, Margaret pulled from the pocket at the back of her mind the impression she had received that Jane was already acquiring the ghost-mask.

"Do you think Aunty is happy there?" she asked Eva.

"Happy? I don't know. Reasonably contented, I would imagine. Happy is a word people use less and less of themselves as they get older, I find. It has a sort of young energetic meaning to it that doesn't go with most people's idea of being past their prime." She laughed. "In some ways she's probably better suited there than she has been since they first came back from India – someone else to do all the chores, all the worrying about little everyday things, while she can concentrate on being lively and amusing and looking smart. Poor Jane, though, I don't envy her – I don't think she's ever really been at peace inside herself.

"I wonder if that's the answer?" Margaret paused while she negotiated a particularly tricky roundabout, and then went on:

"Do you remember the conversation we had before Christmas, when I came for that weekend? I remember you said then about most old people being preoccupied with wondering what it has all been for. And that doesn't make for being at peace with yourself does it?"

"No, and neither does being self-centred. Not many of us, if we're honest, can say we've always lived up to our ideal of ourselves. And if we allow most of our thoughts to be *about* ourselves, well then a good proportion of those thoughts are bound to be uncomfortable."

"I can't imagine your being too uncomfortable, then." Margaret's smile was warm with love and admiration. "I've realised for a long time now that in Eva Bennett's scale of priorities, Eva Bennett has usually been at the bottom."

"Oh come now, don't flatter me, or deceive yourself. I've had my times of selfishness. When your father died, for one. I grieved so much that I wondered whether I'd ever get back on an even keel again. I didn't believe anyone could have suffered as I did. I didn't even take much into account the loss you were feeling. And then I began to tell myself he'd not have thought much of me for caving in, would he? Though if it hadn't been for you I doubt if I'd have come out of it at all. I saw that you needed comfort, too. But that's all past and over these fifteen years and more, although it is connected in a way with what you're saying. It was when I began to get going again that I had to face the fact that I might be going to grow quite old after all, and not slip off after him, as I wanted to at the time."

"I'm very glad you didn't. I'd have missed out on so very much if you had."

"Thank you, love. You know, those of us who've

been lucky enough to have loving and beloved children have a bonus to this business of getting old. You don't believe as I do in some kind of life afterwards, but if you *are* right and I'm wrong, at least we have the joy of knowing that a little bit of us will continue after we're gone, and I'm more sorry than I can ever say that you've not been able to have that comfort."

Margaret did not answer. Old scars still bled on occasion.

They were nearing Eva's home now, and neither of them spoke much until they were in the house.

"It's been a grand day, Meg," said Eva as they sat for the few minutes they had together before Margaret set off for Delton. "One of those times when you seem to move further forward than you were yesterday, and that's always good."

"I'll tell you something – you're a wise old woman!"

"Don't know about that, love. If anyone troubled to ask, I dare say they'd find quite a lot of us old folk would be able to give a helping hand with some kind of problem or another. Only not many do trouble to ask. Most people shy off because they don't seem to want to talk to us about things that really matter, or because they think we can't tell them anything they don't already know. And another thing – how many times have you heard people say 'I hope I don't get like that'? 'Like what?' I want to ask. They so often only see the outside of us, as we begin to break down physically, and they don't seem to realise that there might be something left inside that keeps us all different from one another, with different things to offer."

"Oh, dear, as usual I'd love to stay on and talk more, but I really must be getting back. Early duty tomorrow. You're right, it has been a good day. I only hope you aren't too tired. I'll phone you and let you know what I've decided about the job – though I think I know already what I'm going to do."

They walked together down the garden path which was now reflecting the last golden balm of the setting sun.

"Drive carefully then. And thank you again for taking me to see Jane. I'll have lots to think about, and I'm glad I can picture her there now that I've seen the place. Now sometime before you leave it, if you do, I'd like to come and see Moortop."

"You're one of the few people I know who would probably see what it has in common with Hornlow. I'll try to arrange it soon. 'Bye dear."

During that night George Hancock died. He had been transferred from Barford General to Moortop several weeks previously and despite the best efforts of medical and nursing stuff his slow deterioration had continued. Although Margaret had encountered Alan and Laura on occasion during their visits to his ward, they had maintained a polite distance from her.

Two days later Grace Morley phoned her from the main office.

"Mr and Mrs Hancock wonder if you've got a couple of minutes to spare them. They're here to collect George Hancock's things.

Unsurprised, but mildly wondering at the reason for their request, Margaret offered her sympathy as they came into the room; both their faces showed the strains of something more than the natural grief of bereavement.

"We wanted to say thank you for all you and the nurses did while Dad was here," began Alan. "I know it's your job, but we both feel that there's that little bit extra – not easy to define – that most of the staff do which makes so much difference."

"We try, certainly," Margaret said. "And it's always gratifying when that's recognised. Thank you – I'll tell them on the ward."

"Alan didn't want him to come here, you know. But

we both feel now that it was for the best." Laura looked uncertainly at her husband. There was a pause.

"The thing is," said Alan, "how can anyone be sure what is for the best for anyone when you just can't connect with them? In all these weeks here, and we've visited most days, Dad hardly said a word. He wasn't senile, he was all right mentally right up to the end, but we never talked, not really what I call talked. We could see that all his physical needs were being met far better than we could have managed if he'd been at home. And we often found the staff chatting to him, but I never felt they were getting through to him either. It hurts to think of his last months being a time of such isolation."

"It is hard, I agree." The professional tone was tempered with caring. "I can't pretend that any of us have a comfortable answer to give. In this job we naturally give a great deal of thought to just such matters as you're raising, but none of us, I think, can claim to have come up with cut and dried solutions. Perhaps your father's withdrawing so determinedly was his way of dealing with the prospect of death? Perhaps he felt, too, that that would make it easier for you to let go of him."

Alan sat hunched in his chair, and Laura put a hand on his knee. Then she said:

"When everything's sorted out I'd like to come and talk to you about the possibility of doing some voluntary work here if that would be acceptable?"

"Of course, whenever you feel like it."

This was not the time to talk about her own affairs, to say that she would probably have left Moortop by the time Laura Hancock began the process of trying to rid herself of the burden of her unjustified sense of guilt.

Two good people, she thought, as she shook hands with them. With any luck they'll work this through together and be the better for it. Such strange legacies one generation sometimes leaves to the next.

Home again in Station Street, Flo Spendlove settled back into a precariously independent existence. There were times when a tumble, or a dropped kettle, or being unable to get to the door quickly enough to answer a knock set her stomach a-flutter with the dread that They would come along and say "You can't manage on your own". But she was mostly able, she was sure, to convince Hugh and Linda on their regular calls, and the health visitors who continued to keep an occasional eye on her, that she was coping.

She couldn't be sure what Doctor Bradshaw thought, but she was sometimes caught out by Norah Goodwin, who popped over most days on her way to or from her domestic job at Moortop. Norah wasn't easy to fool, and she felt a special kind of friendship with her now, after the way she'd been so kind in hospital. That made it harder not to confide in her too much, not to let her see how difficult she found it to keep going calmly when she'd done something silly like not quite turning the gas tap right off, or like last week, not being sure which day it was and not having her shopping list ready for Linda.

What she missed most from the life before she'd been ill was Maureen. Time after time she tried to think what she could have said or done to turn the girl against her. True, Maureen had been to see her once or twice while she'd been staying at Hugh's, and once since she'd come back here. But each time Maureen had been edgy; even – though Flo didn't like to think the word about her dear granddaughter – false. She never stayed long, and didn't appear interested in anything Flo had to talk about, and yet she didn't have much to say about her own doings either. And Hugh and Linda didn't seem to want to talk about her.

One Tuesday when Linda came for the pension book, she said: "Maureen rang last night. She asked me to give you the news. She and Colin Wilkinson were married on Saturday in a registry office near where Colin works, in the south. They'll be living down there, so I don't suppose we'll see much of her in future."

There were so many questions Flo wanted to ask, but Linda's expression and manner discouraged them, so she said simply:

"Well, now, I hope they'll be very happy. You'll let me have their address, won't you? I'd like to send them a present, if you can suggest something you think they need. Or I could send some money, if not."

"If you really want to, of course that's your business, but I think she's treated all of us very badly, especially you..."

"Don't let's talk any more about it. I'd sooner not. Just give me the address sometime."

It wasn't until much later that they both realised that for the first time since her stroke, Flo's speech throughout this exchange had been clear and firm and unhesitant.

When Linda had left, Flo permitted herself a few tears, although she could not have said who she was really crying for. By the sound of it Maureen was going to have a baby and even though it had meant a hasty wedding it should still have been a cause for family rejoicing. Instead, here was Linda – and probably Hugh too – feeling bitter and vengeful, herself sad and more lonely than ever, and who knew what the girl herself was feeling? Life was a funny old business and she wasn't sure she wanted much more of it, all things considered. Still, she'd better put the kettle on; she supposed Linda would expect the usual cup of coffee when she came back with the pension money.

As a witness at Colin's wedding Martin had been one of only very few people present from Delton. Even Maureen's parents hadn't gone, though Colin's Mum and Dad had been there. He returned home to find Edna in a state of agitation.

"On the table – that long envelope. It's your results,

isn't it?"

She stood slightly apart from him as he slit the flap, watching his face closely, preparing herself for whatever response might prove to be appropriate.

"Ah well, that's it then." He tried to assume a disappointed expression, but she saw his eyes laughing.

"Come on, Martin, don't fool about. What've you got?"

He passed the sheet to her.

"Could have done better, but not much, actually. It's enough to get me in and that's what matters."

She hugged him and said:

"Well done, love. You deserve it, the way you've worked this year. Congratulations. Go and ring your Dad – he was all for staying off work this morning to wait for you getting back to open it."

During a celebration meal in the Crown hotel in Barford that evening, Martin said:

"This seems the right time to say thanks to both of you. You're pretty good parents, you know. Not easy to say, this, but your support's meant a lot and I may not always have shown how much I appreciate it. End of speech. No more. Let's have another bottle, shall we? Got to get used to booze if I'm going to be a medical student."

Edna and Arnold looked at each other. Arnold said:

"Thanks son. I'll only say we're proud of you."

"Now, tell us about the wedding. Did you find out why Maureen's parents didn't go?"

"Obvious, isn't it? You know Mr and Mrs Spendlove. Maureen hasn't hit it off with them for ages, and I suppose having to get married finished her with them. Rotten shame, I think. But she doesn't seem to mind – she's a lot harder than she used to be. She and Colin seem to be OK though, so I guess it'll turn out all right. I do hope so. Colin's a bit of an ass, but he's a good type really.

"It's a pity they couldn't enjoy a few years before

having that responsibility." Edna looked across the table at Martin. "But that's their affair, and it's all so different nowadays. Just you watch you don't..."

Martin cut her off:

"Hey, don't come the conventional middle-class Mum with me. I hope I'm not that stupid, but even if it did happen, so what? Life's changing. We don't see it as a disaster, a disgrace, any more. And it's going to change a lot more in the future. Don't you witter about me. I'll be a good boy, I promise, and – what is it Grace Morley is always saying?" He mimicked Grace's voice: "If I can't be good I'll be careful!"

Edna tried to look suitably shocked but the unaccustomed amount of wine released her laughter to join with theirs.

Chapter 14

It didn't take long for the news to spread that Margaret Bennett had turned down the offer of the Matron's job on a permanent basis. Grace was first with the details in the main office.

"She's going to take a Tutors' course. Seems a funny decision at her age, going back to being a student when she could have been the king-pin here and then moved on somewhere bigger if she'd wanted to."

"Maybe she's had enough of Moortop," said Beryl. "Anyway, she'd make a good teacher, and then there's all this re-organisation coming. I wouldn't want to face that if I were in charge here."

"You can say that again. Do any of us? It's not going to be so matey here when that happens – all these new names for everyone, managers for this and heads of that – it'll be more like some ruddy department store. I might even get out myself when it happens."

"That'd be the day." Beryl knew Grace very well. "You'll be here until you retire, you mark my words."

"Perish the thought! Hey, I wonder if Margaret Bennett is thinking of having a farewell party? If she doesn't say anything by next week, we'll arrange one for her whether she likes it or not."

Before finally accepting the offer of a place on the course, which was due to start in November, Margaret carefully traced the process by which she had arrived at her decision. She was in no doubt that one of the most potent elements in her desire to teach was a form of sublimation for the missed experience of motherhood. But there had to be much more than that, otherwise ultimately, anything she might have to give would be spurious, even at worst betrayal.

Her thoughts ranged over her talks with Martin, her contacts with some of the newly-qualified nurses, her observations of the twisted personalities of women like Martha; and the memories of a long-ago succession of unsatisfying relationships following Brian's death. She saw that all these things, too, had contributed in some measure.

You had to believe in yourself, in your capabilities, in the value of what you'd learned from life for its own sake; and yet somehow remain humble enough to want to go on learning. Hopefully the demands of a new period of study (though admittedly these were not likely to prove too challenging) would keep those factors in proportion. And if in the end it all turned out to have been a mistake?

She remembered a conversation with Laura and Alan Hancock – all very well to preach at other people about guilt being counter-productive, not so easy to avoid self-blame when one made one's own errors. She would just have to cope with that too, if it happened. It wouldn't be the first time she'd made a faulty judgment, but about this one she felt almost wholly positive. She sealed the envelopes containing her resignation from Moortop and her acceptance of the course offer, and took them to the post.

The only person to whom she would have been prepared to make any justification would have been her mother, but when she phoned, Eva asked for none, saying simply: "I'm glad you're going to do it." To anyone else who asked "Why?" she answered, "Because I want to."

Eighteen months in post, even at a senior level, didn't qualify Margaret for much in the way of an official leaving celebration. But when they looked back over the short period of her stay at Moortop most members of the staff agreed that she'd be very much missed, and willingly fell in with Grace's proposal that she should be given a lively send-off.

"Nothing very formal," Grace told her, tongue-in-cheek. "Just a few of us for a bit of a knees-up and some nosh. We wondered if you'd like to ask your mother to join us, if you think she'd enjoy it."

"That's a very kind thought. Yes, I've been wanting for some time to bring her down here, and as this will be my last chance I'll take you up on it."

"Friday night, then, about half-seven. I've fixed it with Mr Barraclough that we can have the hall."

Margaret met Eva off the early afternoon train and took her for a short ride round Delton, and then drove up the lane. As they neared the entrance Margaret pointed out the top of the bell-tower above the trees.

"It's a lovely setting," said Eva, "but I should imagine in the old days it would have seemed a very isolated and rather forbidding kind of place."

"That was the idea once upon a time. I hope we're finally managing to change the picture, although do you know there are still a few people in Delton who talk about The Union, even after all this time."

Eva had noticed the "we".

"I think you're going to miss it all in some ways, aren't you?" she asked as they got out of the car and walked up to Margaret's flat.

"Yes, I shall. It'll be strange not to be in any kind of authority for a bit, but I think what I'll miss most is the feeling of belonging which most people here seem to have. These places really are little communities all on their own, and it's almost like being part of an extended family. Even the misfits are there, like in most families."

She filled the electric kettle.

"Now come along, sit down and put your feet up for a few minutes while I make a cup of tea. Then we'll have a walk round so that you can get some idea of the people and places I've talked about. Even though I'm leaving so soon, it won't be as pointless as it might seem because I think you'll be able to see even more clearly why I want to take up this next challenge."

"Oh, Meg, you're so like your father in some ways. He was never so happy as when he felt he'd got a worthwhile cause to work at!"

The buzz of noise they could hear as they approached the hall at half-past seven sounded anything but "just a few of us", and us they went in through the door Margaret had to admit that she'd been completely taken in by Grace's understatement. She wondered whether there were any staff at all left on the wards, so many seemed to be gathered here, among them even one or two who'd retired during her time; Dr Rayner and his wife, Martin and his parents, domestics, porters – everyone Grace could think of had been invited, and most had responded. In one corner sat a little group of residents, Anne Prince in their midst clutching a box of chocolates on her lap. As Margaret walked down the hall, Anne got up and rushed towards her, thrusting the box at her as Eddie whistled her on.

"For you, best wishes from us all in The House," she said, thus ruining Grace's carefully prepared sequence of events. The idea had been that the residents' little presentation would be included in the general informal speech-making later in the evening. But no-one really minded, and the incident broke the ice with a sudden warmth.

The party was one about which Grace would say many times in the future to new members of staff who were yet to come: "Ah, but you should have been here when Margaret Bennett left. That was a do to remember."

Doctor Rayner, at Grace's request, presented Margaret with the collective gift of a set of crystal wineglasses, and his brief remarks were made directly to her rather than to the company.

"I thought you were making a mistake to go, and that your looking after Moortop was the best contribution you had to offer. I know now I was wrong. We all hope that in the future what you do will be properly appreciated. Our affection and our good wishes go with you."

When Grace then began to speak, Martin crossed his fingers in expectation of an anti-climax. In fact what she said was shrewd, witty and sincere, and he joined enthusiastically in the applause.

By ten o'clock the party was an assured success and Grace, dancing with Martin, shouted above the volume of the music and the general hubbub:

"When you're famous, I'll be able to say that I once twisted with you!"

Later still, when one or two of the auxiliaries began to show signs of excessive merriment Margaret thought briefly of Irene Gifford, and wondered what her future held. Until replacements for both Irene and herself had been officially appointed, Sister Hemsley was to be temporarily in charge, and Margaret made time to have a quiet word with her.

"Don't hesitate to give me a ring, if things get on top of you," she told her. "I'm quite confident you'll cope, but sometimes it's a bit lonely being in the place where, to coin a phrase, the buck finally stops. And if you do decide to apply for the Deputy job, of course I'll back you unreservedly."

The usual promises were made as the party ended, to "keep in touch"; if any one of them were kept, she believed that it would be Martin's. After so many leave-takings in her life, she knew that very few work-based relationships lasted once the link had broken. There was always a slight sense of betrayal on both sides – whether you were the one moving on or one of those left behind. But she had the feeling, as she shook Martin's hand, that there would be a re-acquaintance one day.

The following morning as she and her mother were

having an early breakfast in the flat where Eva had spent the night, they agreed that perhaps the nicest thing of all about the party had been the huge spray of flowers which Grace had given to Eva during the celebrations.

"That little gesture says a lot about these people," said Eva. "The place may be no Hornlow Hall, but they do seem to try to make it a bit more than just your famous mental waiting room."

"Not enough of them, and not effectively enough," said Margaret. "And that won't change until a lot of other things have – attitudes, beliefs, expectations. That's what I want to help to do. I've got no illusions, mind. I quite expect that when my own turn comes to be old, I'll have no idea whether or not I've made the slightest pinprick of an impact. And maybe in twenty years from now the problems could even be worse. But once you think you can do something, however little, you've got to try, haven't you?"

Eva nodded. "Yes, dear, you've got to try."

"The Union"

The very early beginnings of the workhouse in England started with the Poor Law Act of 1388. This was passed to help deal with the labour shortages caused by the Black Death plague, by limiting the movement of labourers.

One of the outcomes of the Act was that the state, in the form of individual parishes, became responsible for the maintenance of the poor. In the early part of the nineteenth century the number of paupers was growing rapidly, largely as a result of changes in farming, industry and trade. Many of the parishes were struggling to meet their commitments.

In 1834 the Poor Law Amendment Act was passed and the parishes were amalgamated into Unions charged with administering poor relief. A workhouse was built in each Union, and the intention was that aid was only to be given to paupers who entered the workhouse. Before this time "parish poor relief" was mainly given in the form of money or goods, although smaller workhouses did exist.

The intention of the Union workhouses was to discourage claims on the poor relief system. Life inside the workhouses was deliberately made unpleasant, so that only those in desperate need would enter them.

This is why "The Union" was so feared. Those who had nowhere else to turn, faced separation from spouses and children, hard monotonous work, poor food and general degradation.

In 1930 the Union Boards were disbanded and their responsibilities were taken over by Local Authorities. Many of the workhouses were renamed as Public Assistance Institutions. They carried on housing those who were not able to fend for themselves, the long-term sick, the elderly, unmarried mothers and other unfortunates.

The National Assistance Act of 1948, Part III, referred to the duty of provision of residential accommodation by Local Authorities. This became known as Part III accommodation.

The totally fictional "Moortop" of this story describes one such example of a workhouse. In the period described in "This Way Out"(1960s and 1970s) the inmates, males and females in separate areas, were housed in Part III accommodation.

Several hospital wards held the sick or severely handicapped, and by the early twentieth century an area of the top floor held any "fallen women" with their illegitimate offspring until the babies were taken away for adoption. These women were often then housed in Part III accommodation, where, in many cases, they would spend the rest of their lives.

By the late 1980s most "workhouses" had gone, to be replaced by modern care homes.

Printed in Great Britain
by Amazon.co.uk, Ltd.,
Marston Gate.